I0686853

Grind Show Editions

Western Roads

Michael Joseph Walsh was born on January 13, 1960 in Buffalo, New York of Irish, German, and Italian ancestry. Walsh was a rebellious and adventurous youth, leaving Minneapolis for Florida at nineteen. He hitchhiked frequently, and journeyed to San Diego, California soon after he turned twenty, where he spent six years working as a construction laborer. Walsh resided in California for eighteen years; also living in Sacramento and the San Francisco Bay Area.

In 1995, Walsh graduated *with distinction* from California College of Arts and Crafts (now called California College of the Arts) in Oakland. The following year Walsh created the book titled *Graffito*, a photo essay of the graffiti phenomenon in the San Francisco Bay Area. The book was well received in the United States and Europe.

Walsh ventured to Prague, Czech Republic in 1997 and began work on *Frontier Town*, a photo essay which explores the remnants of Soviet communist rule and occupation in Prague. For the next year he traveled the city extensively by tram and subway with his camera. *Frontier Town* is scheduled to be published in 2014-15.

In 1998 Walsh's work in Prague was cut short when he was awarded a Fulbright Scholarship in Photography to Taiwan. That fall Walsh arrived in Taipei and began work on a capacious photo essay of Taiwanese culture later titled *Shangri-la Motel* (unpublished). In 2011, *Cadillac Fin Suitcase* was published, a collection of short stories set in Taiwan. Walsh lives with his wife, Julia (Mei-Hsiang) Wu.

Also by Michael Walsh

Graffito
Cadillac Fin Suitcase

Western Roads is a Grind Show Editions book / In association with Frontier Drifter Productions

Western Roads is a work of fiction. All characters appearing in this work are fictitious. Any resemblance to real persons, either alive or dead, is purely coincidental.

Copyright © 2013 by Michael Walsh
All rights reserved. This complete work is registered with the US Copyright Office. No part of this book may be reproduced in any form or by any electronic or mechanical means, including information storage and retrieval systems without permission in writing from the author, except by a reviewer, who may quote brief passages in a review.

ISBN-13: 978-0-615-80274-9   ISBN-10: 0615802745

This book is dedicated to the memory of my father, Dr. John Walsh, who overcame hard times as a child and young man, and lived life with integrity, perseverance, and courage.

Western Roads

At fourteen I began hitching county roads west of Minneapolis—after discovering Sheila Pierre and the way of the bhang pipe. The tar roll was my *sanctuaire*. My muse. My mentor. Passage to the bright midnight's pageant of actors, scenes—and I got to play a part. My brain fizzed when brake lights flashed. The driver—a bon bon? A slug of vinegar?—I didn't care. Looted every ride—took a tale, a look, a dialect. I was bulletproof! Slippery as a fish! My life an opera of revolt. Soliloquy of hot obsidian. I was vaporous! Castigated! Bloody as Delacroix's palette knife! I bashed drums. Danced around fires screaming incantations! Illuminations! Wanderlust ripped velvet from my antlers. My kid wings dragged in slush. High school administrators dogged me. Wanted to smote all judges! Serpents of Gestalt! I was charmed by wolves! Rimbaud! Blake! Masturbated to California maps. Hobo trains spooked in my gut. Coal furnaces crammed with church flowers and holiday pigs. Whistles rioted! Conductors were jettisoned! Western Union telegraph wires hummed along weed highways: FRONTIER AWAITS STOP LEAVE NOW STOP REBEL SONS OF THE WEST. At fourteen I threw haymakers at the sun! Pissed Molotov! Could hump state line in an hour flat! Longed for heroic parades. Ribbons! An opus! Some kids squeezed Jesus. Some, booze. I needed to move!

Sheila was fifteen. My wolf girl! Fortune-teller! Erato! Chilled off my boyhood with French kisses, lessons in "going steady." We had sex for three months—a series of clumsy electrocutions. She was the first. On Memorial Day she quartered me. Stuffed me into her Easy Bake Oven. Cranked it. I hitched five miles to St. Louis Park. Two a.m. Juiced. Vas deferens poised. Brain flickering Swedish Erotica. Crowed at her window. Her pap awoke—half gargoyle!—half Baptist!—drooling nitric! Swinging a Louisville Slugger! Hunted me for two blocks. I shinnied up a willow. Switched off the sound. The brute U-turned back to the house, took long sloppy bites out of Sheila—her friend told me. Never saw her again.

Getting unloaded mutilated my pride but barely bruised my heart. There'd be a stringer of others. My best girl wore diesel. Steamy asphalt ribbons poured over her gravel shoulders. Curves that took me to Zanzibar.

I hitched alone or with Othello Bolen. My Tom Sawyer! My confederate. My mulatto. Half James Langston Hughes, half James Dean. A few of us at Arm & Hammer High kept his secret. The school was half-full of Candy Land racists! Republican larva! Slanderers! Othello the swashbuckler! The peacock! The sultan of social intercourse! Seldom seen without his Kentucky coonskin cap. Wore it to school dances. Wore it to juvie. Wore it the night he screwed Principal Shultz's wife at the Hi-Lo Motel. We called him Scout. He sprouted muscles, started shaving in sixth grade. And scoring beer at Glen Lake Liquor for high schoolers. Othello tossed his razor out on Wednesdays. Fridays and Saturdays after slop, with goat stubble and a wad of ones, he'd ride his Schwinn Sting-Ray into town. Nicked two bucks per buy. In the black! Double Eagles! Rhino gravy! Swarmed by heels-and-pie (Othello's harem begins)! Liquor store owner raked it in, too. He tossed

Scout a twelve-pack every weekend.

Lauded, "Hey! That's my flimflam!"

Scout propped his father, Reginald "Reggie" Bolen on a pedestal. Shined his ass from a step ladder. Reggie did a ten spot at Honeywell. Cognitive Purge Inspector for a deuce. Intravenous Mercury Coordinator on a top-secret aerospace project. Then they sent him a pink paper airplane. Hung himself in the garage a month later, on the Fourth of July. Seven-year-old Othello found him. Reggie's swinging feet flicked the sugar off the kid. He hacked his hair off. Waved a pocket knife on the playground.

His mother was Florence Gautier. Almighty Flo. Seeping Angie Dickinson. Perpetually puffy-eyed. Fur drool. I'd always wanted to fluff Flo. She tanked the martini shaker after Reggie swung. Skidded along the cocktail-party circuit. Toured between Benzedrine and Cocksucker. They soon cut Havana, Illinois, for Minneapolis.

Scout was supposed to tell everyone that his (white) daddy, a highly decorated colonel, was KIA in Viet Nam.

Othello hated Flo for that.

2

September '74. Jerry Ford appointed. Tricky Dick, the anointed—pardoned for pissing all over Lady Liberty's gown. Cries for a pinching, cries for a lynching were met without a sound. Inside the Beltway, there was a melee. Elephant tusks strewn all over the ground. On our block, Billy the Eagle Scout blew his brains out. Said his country had let him down. I was beyond the sprinkles of saints. At night, in bed, riffs swarmed—Freddie King, Beelzebub, Hendrix shot me full of holes. Rock 'n' roll wasn't enough. I cracked pane, ignited a toxic. Drooled. Smirked. Dilated. A killer inside me kindled. Miming Hiroshima, teary ballerinas. He dialed Castro. Pled for air support. AK-47s. Tawny whores. Fidel promised Whitehouse schematics. Automatics. A hundred K to Line up Dick, his toads. Blindfolds. Customary cigs. Rat! Tat! Tat!

October. A black-and-blue Saturday. Sifted Sheila's pom pom dust. Jerked off. I was buggy. Ugly. Boozing. Pining for Clearasil. A new god. Picked up the horn. Blew Othello's.

"Atomic number sixteen," he sang, flaunting his science

chops.

"A hitch, Sulfur Boy?"

"Well, uh huh, hee hee," he buttered James Dean. "Mecca?" Meant *Where we going?*

"Spiders from Mars." Meant hitching with no destination—to meet Looney Tunes, feel the sting of the unknown.

"Reckless," he whispered, a taunt. "Still bleeding it off twice a day?"

"With your mother."

"I've got a eureka for tonight's show," his voice puffed with pride.

"What?"

"Memphis Kane."

Demigod. Mutineer. Avant-garde. 170 IQ. 170 arrests. 170 electroshock sessions.

"Really?" I blurted, astonished.

The line went cold.

The show would be buzzing at Radio Dada, our main pirate radio hideout—an abandoned aquarium shop on Purgatory Creek, five volts from home. An erotic cathedral. Sanctuary for libertines, apprentices of lust, slayers of the sacred. Our troupe had broadcast live every Saturday night for the past year using Othello's dad's ham radio. We changed venues often—FCC agents were hot, but we were phantoms. Anonymous. Schoolmates didn't even know our identities. Transmissions were spontaneous—shows featuring bullhorns, kazoos, lithium voice-changers. Black comedy skits. Provocations of revolution. Civil disobedience. Readings from William Burroughs, Blake, Baudelaire. Initiation: memorize Hugo Ball's Dada manifesto. Recite it in public, naked. A juvie record got a kid in automatic.

An hour churned. I was stuffed with stray dogs. Baling wire. Strangled corpses of kings. Burned a J behind our house. Visions of Othello, gloating over his prize, Memphis Kane. Viceroy of the Blue Monkey band of activists, saboteurs who'd dropped scorpions in Sam's bed. My favorites: Five birthday cakes stolen from the Nevada Test Site, plutonium sucked; the dental facility burgled, hot metal swapped for silver used for amalgams. And the turning of Big Betty, wife of the Secretary of the Interior, concerning leukemia kids living in high-fallout areas of Utah. Big sang at a Senate moo-maw after receiving flicks of her daddy tonguing twats at a Toledo motel. Blue Monkey tripped trains toting war teeth. Sabotaged eco-asshole factories in Cal. Exposed NYC sweatshops. Protested everywhere, NSEW. Memphis and company evoked Don Quixote. Sitting Bull. Spartacus. Possibility of Earth without governments, guns, money. A siting required a genuflection. A repudiation. A contemplation.

I obsessed about alleged markings on Memphis's body: Yakuza tattoos, third-degree burns, Swastikas, scars from the Korean conflict, suction divots from a giant squid. Some graped he was a CIA spook. Tuned his pecker KGB. Last year, in town, he forfeited a femur in a car wreck trying to run down Ringtone, his ex. For years she'd cut up the hogs— brought home slabs of Hormel. Memphis spent *buku* time in the VA nut wing, jail, court. Ringtone tired. Tossed him. He seeped into a crackerbox on Shit Street. Kept Glen Lake Liquor in the black. Cruised town in a psychedelic Toronado ragtop with his radical recordings blaring. Memphis *was* the counterculture in town. Bluebirds, church groups, the Rotary Club had failed to run him off.

Six p.m. Moon bloodied the sun's nose. I burned down the long fuse, tucked it into my roach can. Lit out for Radio Dada, down Westmill Road—my street—lined with tract homes— desperation—factory cadets. Eyes watched me. Informants. The righteous. Houses pinched in like a scrap-metal crusher. Bang! Groan! Scrape! I loathed myself. My street. Lie! Some neighbors were cool. And the Montclairs next door and Rogers across the street were aces.

I blurred legs half a mile to County Road 3. Memphis Kanes's Toronado asleep on the shoulder. I crossed into woods, skipped Dick-and-Jane on a forgotten dirt road leeching Purgatory Creek, a Frank Zappa jingle away from Radio

Dada. A raven swooped overhead. Sure sign of bad luck! Weird scenes invaded my View-Master. Cactus jacks. Towering Barbarella. Ground covered with batts of pink Owens-Corning fiberglass insulation. Pop footage spun—last time I'd seen a raven, he'd walloped me good. My moxie gasped! I ran for asylum. Would he be waiting up tonight? Two weeks prior, I jittered in the kitchen. On the red X. The wallop spot. Brownies in slippers and cowboy pajamas dodged me, carrying cakes of wet plaster and gunpowder. The old man at the table in a T-shirt and shiver-me-timbers trousers. Buddy Holly's stout twin. Working over a bottle of Irish Mist. He looked at me. The V stare splattered on the wallpaper behind me. He made the sign of the cross. For him? For me? It didn't matter! With a boy in the crosshairs it always meant, on the morrow, a freshly skinned buffalo rotting in the sun on the grassy plain. My knees banged an Our Father! Footsteps upstairs. The Tooth Fairy waiting for business? Mom and kids stacking sandbags? The floorboards were piano keys playing the *Night of the Hunter* songbook.

Two brownies teetered over carrying Pop's favorite invention: "The Inquisitor." Cerebellum probes jutted out. Goddamn IRA birthday candles! The brownies shoved me into the strap-o-lounger. Slapped the crown on my head. Now he had me! Pop served his Belfast grin. The one he kept under the stairs in a violin case. No one outside the family ever saw it. I was a wooden leg hanging on a Peace Wall. My head spun like a busted carousel. Looking for exits. A rat hole! A sewer hole! I'd chew through drywall to slobber on Liberty's boob job. Waited for his first words. Always the same droll greeting before unchaining the wolf. Time crawled! A Gila monster on the Devil's belly. Anemic kids wearing potato-sack dresses clobbered the door—waiting for my organs for transplant.

"Hello, frieeeeeend," Pop finally purred and threw down the Inquisitor's switch.

The Gila monster turned to dust! My crown lit up, blinked and blew like a bug-eyed sermon-steaming preacher. I gnawed caribou antlers. Blubbered phony prayers in Latin and Czech!

Pop was going to pry me open like a mule's rocker panel. He held up The Hands! Twice the normal size! I imagined The Hands squeezing cuckoo out of my throat! The old man jiggled coins in his pocket. Another sign that all fuck was about to break loose!

"Let's have it, Mucklebird." His voice a guttural sea.

"The church has it ass-backward," I said brashly, egging him on.

His boiler ruptured. Fried his voice box. I almost had him now! Up on my rocking horse—begging for a haymaker.

"The church's 'sex is bad, violence is good' has always seemed goddamned cross-eyed to me."

Pop sprang off his cathedra. "Like it or lump it," he crowed and hurled a plate of chuck roast and potatoes past my head.

He pounced. An open hand caught my pie hole. I went flying. Shit my boxers. The boil-over and chase. I ditched outside into a meteor storm. Bled a mile to Othello's house. Starka vodka. 16mm porn. Two hours foamed. My mother strode up the drive. My *illuminato!* Joan of Arc! Me and Pop's long-suffering mediator. She wore seraph wings. The door buzzed.

I jellied toward it, shouted, "Kill it."

Othello oscillated in front of the screen, *Deep Throat* burning his naked torso. "Reckoning! Reckoning!" he tee-heed, ran, cut the projector.

I opened the swinger. A breaker of Starka rushed out. Joan floated above it. Above everything. She was regal. Immaculate. Sagacious.

"Hello, friend," I slurred.

She laughed.

"Goddamnit," I drawled, rubbed my red cheek.

"I know."

"I asked for it."

"We can watch *Laugh-in* with the other kids. I made popcorn. Come on."

I grinned, gave her a wink, trudged to the waiting Galaxie 500. Othello, in the window, mimed a hanging.

Pop was a Cortland, New York, beauty. John G., a Depression-era kid. An orphan gutted by the spade he used to bury his folks. His father when he was eleven. Mother, fourteen. He worked in a charcoal factory and bowling alley through high school. Mom told me. Pop never uttered a single word about his parents. Pop's metamorphosis—courage of Lugh. Teeth of a lion. Bum elbow from shaking his fist at the world. TB at twenty-three. MD at twenty-eight. Celtic boxers, Irish Rovers on the phonograph. Johnny Marzetti and Pabst Blue Ribbon. Pop was our sovereign! Our orator! Proclaiming the glory of Canisius College, his alma mater! Jesuits! Nailed Irish House of Lords edicts into our foreheads—I had scars for every saint!

I continued to lope. Night bullied. Moon creamed the sun. Landscape calcified. Black. Monstrous. Crustacean. The road ended, hurling me into a meadow. I squelched the gasp machine. Dropped testicles. Walked hi-ho. Radio Dada!—a hundred feet ahead, squeezing Purgatory Creek's nearly barren breast. Only structure in sight. Black lights, glowing ominously on the facade, illuminated fluorescent-blue paint we'd smeared on the bricks. "Radio Dada," spelled out in pieces of scrap metal Othello had twisted in shop class, hung from the gutter above the hive hole. I marched up to bee butter. Felt pathetic. Tingly. Memphis Kane was inside!

I picked up a gallon can of gas, topped off the portable generator, called out, "Man Ray," our signal. It echoed back.

I pricked the Visqueen door, bled down a dark canal, toward a reptile's womb. Treasonous bombasts scored the walls. Hefty Bags loaded with dismembered mannequins lined the walls. Heads jutted out, each of our father's names in white spray paint. The aisle foamed me to our idol, a urinal, our rendition of Marcel Duchamp's *Fountain 1917*. We never peed in it. Gilded it with phony roses.

I heard Othello moan. I sidestepped *Fountain*. Othello on the Marshmallow sofa, Memphis Kane giving him head. I crimsoned. Halted. Othello gave me a wink, fluttered Pharaoh's eyes. Memphis caught sperm. Arose Osiris. Turned, faced me, simpered. Scout squirmed, zipped fish. I studied our hero. Come-and-get-it eyes. Bedpan jaw. Goatee. Burroughs' suit. Wondered which leg was phony. I stayed cryogenic.

"You a blast-zone boy?" droned Memphis. His eyes swiped my cardboard cutout.

"Fresh out of zoa," I bawled, strode within ten feet of him, stopped. "MSM's cool," I said, "but I don't partake." Was this Scout's first blue, I pondered?

Memphis smiled, bowed. Wiped cum. Torched a Marlboro.

Othello mimed jerking off, sparked a Bubonic, blew a Hell's rainbow. "It ain't homosexual, Mike," a whine of frustration in his voice. "It's all part of the great paradisiacal awful goddamn experiment. Since when did the Wanderer draw boundaries?" he asked rhetorically, jumped up, handed me the blunt, clamped on drywaller stilts leaning against Marshmallow, lunged in circles. "I'm a hurly-burly whirly!" he bellowed.

I dragged the Bubonic, woke six lava lamps perched on a smut bookcase, eyed my pal. He looked sharp in a Davy Crocket jacket with fringed sleeves, woolies, and his trademark coonskin.

"Grab some duds, judge," he laughed, flipped me off. "This is a roly-poly holy historic occasion!"

I walked to the clothes rack—Halloween outfits, ratty furs, dresses, thrifty store suits and old man duds some of our paps had coughed up. Coats, dress pants and suspenders, hats and ties. I threw on a baggy gray suit coat, salmon Fedora.

Othello clomped past. "Spiffy," he heckled, mimed *up yours*.

I rewound, *Since when did the Wanderer draw boundaries?* I smelled Vaseline. Erotic fantasies whirred. Dobermans fucking trailer trash. Ivory cocks. Midget threesomes. "Scout's got the pulse," I told myself. His trying queer was no big deal. But the surprise of it kept coldcocking me.

Memphis fanned peacock feathers. "What time we ring-a-ding-ding?"

I found dry land on Marshmallow, pulled a Miller from a twelve-pack Othello had probably stolen from his mom, cracked it, killed half. "Seven. No condom, no diaphragm," I shot.

"Peachy." He ambled to the ham setup on a workbench kissing the back wall, perched on a stool in front of the mic, torched another nail.

"You got thirty, forty minutes tops," I said. "Longer and someone might trace our sparks."

"I told him," cried Othello as he crashed around Marshmallow, dropped next to me.

"Raven nicked me on the way over," I whispered in his ear. "We better torpedo the show."

He stroked his coonskin's tail. "Superstitious," he blared, then shrunk, whispered back, "You understand about what I did, uh before, don't you?"

"Uh-huh."

He smiled.

"Man Ray," chirped a voice from outside.

I hailed. Two of our tyros appeared, Icee Bad Water and Zobar. Slave boys who showed potential for illustrious acts of chaos. Degradation. Icee was Cherokee—recently dropped minnows in a cougar of fourteen. Coupon abortion. Rock-salt gossip. Father O'Doud's penance of thumbscrews, rectory chores, ice age of cold showers, improved the punk's chances of becoming a Radio Dada member. Zobar. Gregarious. Albanian. The "Human Megaphone." Could only keep a secret with a Tirana heater shoved in his yap. We sat on him hard. His papa was a shrink. His ma was in a nut house. Zobar got into fights at school defending her honor. This brought him our unequivocal respect, but we never let on.

Othello jumped up, stomped to the recruits, shook his thumb toward Memphis Kane's back, pomped, "Ready for Godzilla. Spiderman. Batman. Any man!"

Memphis spun around.

"Genuflect," commanded Scout. They did.

Memphis nodded at the fledglings.

Icee eyed the stilts, winked, flashed a wanton smile. "You could spoon cheese out of the Fifty-Foot Woman."

Hyena yips.

"Whoop! Whoop! Whoop!" blipped Zobar, imitating

Curly of the Three Stooges.

Icee asked, "Where's everyone?"

"Cricket, Sly, Pickles, and Jerry are at the sock hop," I said. *"All-Star Wrestling* for Bear, Peanut, and Bullwinkle."

Icee studied Memphis, blurted, "Helmut Luger says he has a nude picture of you."

"Shut up!" screamed Othello, his glare failing to melt Icee.

"Charges a fin a look," smacked the rube. "Fucker hauled in fifty skins last week."

"See it?" chuckled Memphis.

"No, but Sticky Nelson did. Said your skin is sick with silver scales."

Memphis dropped trou. Porpoise bobbing. No scales. "Look like this?" he asked.

"Man! No!" Icee screeched.

Everyone laughed. Memphis pulled up his trousers. I was disappointed his pants hadn't dropped enough to sport Captain Ahab.

I ran outside to fire the generator. Scout followed, dashed past me into moonlight, spun three times, tore off his coonskin, pranced in a circle feigning he was riding a horse.

"This is some high living, hey!" he foamed proudly while continuing to bug around, whipping his hip with the coonskin. "Memphis Kane! Here! And, I bagged him myself."

"You two do any bagging before tonight?" I teased, crouched over the generator.

"Nah. Like I said, carnal combusted spontaneously."

I raised an eyebrow. "A straight seduction? Really?"

"I've been pestering him for weeks to do a show. Okay, I blistered the odds. A few times I didn't wear boxers under my old Levi's. He got an eyeful of Gibraltar."

I shook my head, chuckled. Scout aped Holy Roller. Tongue wagging. Arms and legs gyrating. I laughed, stood up. He set spurs, rode up, gave me a bear hug.

Othello's crush on life always rocked me. "Spiders from Mars after the show?" I asked.

"Uh-huh."

"Two-to-one Memphis is collecting zoa from the tyros."

We laughed. I sparked the generator. We hustled inside. Memphis was dealing blackjack, showing the boys how to cheat. We threw on hash ventilators, sucked Moody Blues. Memphis sat on the stool in front of the mic. Me on his right, Scout on his left. Icee stood over Scout's shoulder, Zobar over mine. Seven rolled. I ignited ham. The mic whistled. Everyone pricked ears.

"Go," I said.

Scout slid the mic under his chin, stole a harlequin's face, tittered, "Radio Dada. From Earth. Time travelers who got off in the wrong century. Eating the feces of our fathers. We worship the magic of narcotics. Beauty of nomads. Ataraxia of monks. We're tapeworms in the belly of the bourgeois. Ten miles. Screaming new vowels. Catcalls. Vows. Tonight we welcome Memphis Kane, alpha male of Blue Monkey. More than a legend. He's an idea. A spear. A bright shadow." Scout moved the mic in front of Memphis, paused, leaned in, asked mischievously, "Mr. Kane, before you begin, could you name some of your deliciously eclectic occupations?"

Memphis droned, "Easter Bunny. Dynamite fisherman. Drive-thru funeral cashier in Reno. Asshole."

We whistled and clapped.

Memphis torched a roach, blew Elvis, leaned in, honeyed like a lullaby, "I've overcome years of social and institutional conditioning, decades of madness, the Republicans, to transcend the moral plain. Constructs of hubris. Institutions of moral terror. The military. The monetary system." He paused, hit the roach, smiled slyly. "But that's not why you're listening, is it?" he taunted. "All of you want to see it, even if it's seeing with your ears." He turned manic, cackled playfully, slid out of Burroughs' jacket, let it drop on the floor. "I'm privy to the prattle concerning my epidermis."

"Whoa!" howled Icee. "Strip!"

"Fucking do it!" Zobar yelled.

Memphis turned Jerry Lewis. Othello, a nervous Dean Martin. The legend ripped his shirt off. Horrific letters had been branded across his chest and washboard. We shot sideshow stares.

He stood up, wiggled his ass. "East Germany, 1956. It's Russian—the story of a spy."

Nausea put on tap shoes. I eyed my pals. Icee vomited to Leningrad. Then dry heaves sent him to the canvas.

Memphis mimed a bullhorn. "Ready for Marlboro Country?" He spiraled. Star-shaped cig burns marred his back. "A going away present."

"Now, bare your soul," Zobar hooted. "Korea! Korea!" The tyros clapped and whistled, egging Memphis on.

"We want to hear about Korea, Mr. War Hero," Icee gurgled from the canvas.

Memphis deflated, sat back down, fell silent. "You don't," he whispered.

"Fuck, we don't," moaned Icee, resurrected out of puke, took his place next to Scout.

Zobar leaned into the mic, brayed, "Five thousand listeners, Memphis. Five grand. Come on!"

Memphis was gut shot. Waved the white flag. Our tyros reloaded. I had a water pistol.

Memphis fussed, hands trembling, tilted his head way back, shook it slightly. He slid a hand over the mic, turned to Scout, said apologetically, "I didn't take my medicine today. My poles, aurora borealis."

Othello whispered in his idol's ear. I looked at my pal for a sign. Drew my finger across my throat, shrugged. Othello mouthed, "It'll be okay."

Memphis lit a Marb, stated serenely, slowly, "June 1953. A place called Pork Chop Hill. I wore a necklace. Enemy ears. My kills. Tore penises off with Vise-Grips."

Othello sat in shock. His face, Munch's *The Scream*.

"Smoked a lot of heroin," continued Memphis. "Survived alone in a bunker for days. All my pals dead. Drank my own urine. Cannibalized my sergeant. They gave me the Silver Star. Said I was prime for spook detail. I hated Gandhi. Mother Teresa," his voice trailed off. He clenched his fists.

We sat dumbstruck.

Memphis whimpered, began to cry. "My sergeant, I fragged the prick. Had it coming." He took a long drag off the butt, blew nooses, whispered, "When I came back after the war, I killed his wife, too."

We stayed mute.

"Didn't plan it. Visited her to confess, then things went schizo." He slid off his stool, thumped down the reptile's womb. He returned instantly with the gallon can of gas, stopped ten feet in front of us.

"Jesus!" screamed Othello. "What the fuck is that for?"

Memphis lifted the can over his head with one hand. Fished a Zippo out of his pocket with the other.

"It's almost full," I warned.

"No! No!" cried Othello. "Don't do it! Don't do it!" He jumped up, ran toward Memphis.

Memphis sparked Zippo, put on a wild face. Othello froze. Icee began to cry. I sat limp.

Zobar sprung up, ran down the womb. "I'll get help!" he shouted over his shoulder.

"Tell Ringtone I love her," Memphis drawled softly.

He doused himself, torched. Erupted like a January Christmas tree, fell over. Othello grabbed a coat from the clothes rack, pounced, tried to squash the flames. It only fanned them. Memphis was a dead fly. His eyes Xs. Smoke filled the room. I pulled Othello away. Hot vapor chased us outside.

We moped in circles. Waiting for badges. Death. Othello lit a butt, buzzed around like a firefighter wind-up toy. I sat on pallets fifty feet from the hive hole. Smoke fumed. Realized the mic was still on in there. What was it picking up? Memphis Kane's rasping specter, his eyes blown out, groping fingerless for the door? Icee crouched on the creek bank, face in hands, crocodile tears. Clouds gathered. Angels flipped us off. We donned thorns. Othello twisted Icee's head off. They tumbled into Purgatory. Frog spit splashed. Arms, legs flailed. Othello let go. Icee, gasping, wormed into cattails.

"*Vete al diablo,*" rasped Othello as he thundered up the

bank. "Rat, I'll burn your fucking house down."

"Swear I won't." Icee liquefied, puddled, trickled down the trail.

Othello killed the firefighter, wilted next to me. We torched cigs, fidgeted—chumps in a silent horror film—Memphis Kane's ghost lying in wait—sporting a strap-on big as Napoleon. We were see-see Bolsheviks. Neurotic as Nuremburg. Sweating in a tiny concrete room. Condemned to the memory of this night. We donned hash ventilators for another round of Fairyland. It didn't take. In my mind Kane misted— two good legs—immaculate skin—.45s in shoulder holsters. Swore we'd die on a black Sunday. I fretted about Scout. His spring's confetti pigeon shit.

"We're John Doe," I finally said.

"John Dillinger," mumbled Scout. "Blue Monkey, the cops, FCC. Hounds coming."

"Icee and Zobar won't snitch."

Scout rolled his eyes, slapped his woolies. Smoke waned. "We'll tip the fuzz at the payphone at Walgreen's," he said. "We can't let the fucking animals desecrate the body. I'm getting the ham." He stood up, walked toward the hive. "Who knows who Zobar might drag back here," he barked over his shoulder. "You better—"

"Get the antenna."

"Yeah."

"Zobar ran straight home," I yelled. "He's too smart to come back. We'll hide the generator, ditch your sign anyway." I plucked a hammer off the pallets, scaled a drainpipe, pried up the clamp holding the antenna. Othello came out with the ham as I worked on the sign. Twenty minutes later we'd erased all evidence of Radio Dada, hiding the antenna, signage, and generator in the woods skirting the meadow. Othello shoved the ham into a backpack, slung it over his shoulders. We walked silently along Purgatory toward 3. I heard Russian dirges. Gavels. Blue Monkeys filing their teeth. Ruin at Radio Dada. My failure to stop it. Scout's gallantry. Halfway, we hid the ham in an abandoned shed, a usual hiding spot.

"I'm too balled up to go home," I said. "Spiders from Mars?"
Othello signed thumbs up without looking at me.
A butt later we made County Road 3. Flaunted thumbs oriental. I was shaky. Watched Othello stand cocked, gazed with admiration at his Davy Crocket and woolies. He spiraled one-eighty, leered eastward, poised, allegiant, his face belonging on a box of Wheaties. But I knew better. Memphis's scene was killing him.

"We burlesque like Siamese twins no matter what happens," he woofed, slugged my shoulder.

"What'd you whisper to him?"

Othello's chin fell on his breastbone. "Stop," he sighed, shrunk, turned away.

Hitching at night takes pluck. Freaks troll. Felons. Fondlers. Fanatics. Othello had found his cool. I hadn't. We were wired. Tuned to the road. Everything was fucked. Winking headlights. I fired a flashlight, featured our faces. It worked. A Torino Cobra sucked our breath, gnawed fifty feet off the shoulder, laid licorice. We cartwheeled to the blue cheese. Jello tires. Parachute. Under the hood, Frankenstein fucked Louie Armstrong. Passenger door gassed. Venus in a bitty Girl Scout getup. Blondie. Rubbing eighteen. Play-Doh cleavage. Rita Hayworth gams. If Venus was a Girl Scout, I was Philip Marlowe.

She stroked the steering, greased, "Uptown."

We slid in back. She boiled the Daytonas, topped out at sixty in a forty. Photo of a baby on the dash, tinsel frame.

Her eyes fluttered pink butterflies in the rearview. "Where you going?"

"Poach this beast?" Scout mocked, refreshing his tough-guy act, batted his peepers playfully.

"My brother's. Why?"

"It ain't you."

"Oh, really?" Venus smirked, snapped her head around, imitated a blowfish. She turned back, torched a smoke, sang high pitch, "So, gals can't have a hard-on for muscle cars, pretty boy?" She beamed victoriously, sucked her index finger, tapped it on the windshield.

Scout didn't flinch, mad smile, eyeballs rolling for a come-back.

She blew onion rings, ran eyes over our outfits. "Cute."

"I'm Kit Carson," bolted Othello, flapped his bandit's tail. "He's the Wanderer."

"Where you going?" Venus tittered.

"Spiders from Mars," I crooned.

"A club?"

"We're there," said Othello. "You."

"Me?"

"We're protégés of the road. Experientialists."

"Narcissists?"

"Billowing," I said. "You're going to give us something. Every ride does. Something that crawls into the river of our perception."

Venus boarded up her Play-Doh, giggled uneasily. "Your parents hippies?"

Othello and I roared.

"Holy executioner!" rattled Othello. "You'd have to meet his dad."

I torched an Old Gold. "That your kid?"

She rippled cold, punched it. "My son," she finally said with a little laugh, stroked the photo. "He turned three today. He's at his grandma's stuffing his face with birthday cake. I'll be going there later."

"No way," I muttered under my breath, checked Othello.

He looked at me cross-eyed, tossed her a Wiffle ball: "Real nice."

We blew bubbles for half a mile, then went aphonic. I flipped back to the Memphis Kane channel. A test pattern. "You're dead" blinking. Anxiety spun me. I had plastic legs. No tongue. A rash head-to-toe. Kane in a foxhole, naked, delirious, swilling piss Kool-Aid, thumping a human-ear neck-lace. Comrades cut up, their rib eyes, Porterhouses hung on a wire over a fire. Ravens circled. I wanted to go home. To Pop's beautiful barrages. Mom's creamed salt cod! I was done for—prayed for tranquilizers. A pulpiteer. Captain America. I looked out into the night. Blue Monkeys sharpened cutlasses! Crazy silhouettes pulsed under a streetlamp on the fritz—zi-zim—zi-zim. We slipped past. Dracula! The Mummy! The Wasp Woman! They scattered. Glen Lake flickered two furlongs ahead.

"Could we pit up ahead first?" I asked. "We need to diddle Walgreen's payphone."

Venus jilted a red light.

Othello pumped his fist, elbowed me, mouthed, "Wow." I faked fireworks. Kane cut my nose off.

"Hopkins Texaco," she tinkled. "We have a gas card. That okay?"

"Sure," we chimed.

We made Texaco in two jilts and a roadkill. Purred to full service. No gas jockey. Strange. She hopped out, swung Samoas, sashayed inside. We watched the whole show. Othello darted for the conch near the door.

"*Buena suerte,*" I said, lit a butt, leaned against Cobra's hood.

Othello dropped ducats on Memphis Kane. A minute sniffled. Venus barreled out carrying a baby! A Socrates in coveralls blew after her. She made Cobra, jumped in. Othello and I locked eyes. He motioned west, conch banging against his thigh. He ran that way. I went limp. Frankenstein daggered Satchmo. I jumped to the side.

Socrates ripped his beard, flung himself on the hood! "Christ! Stop!" he screamed. "That's my grandson!"

Venus revved it, smoked Daytonas. Socrates fell off curbside, twitched. Cobra vanished. Cars zipped by. He finally got up, bulled toward the pumps like a fat man in a hurricane.

"Mike, come on!" Othello called. I twirled. He waited next to a tree line forty yards away. I lurched backward toward my pal. Socrates's eyes bit me.

"We don't know her," I shouted. "Picked us up hitching."

Socrates outstretched his hands, closed in from thirty feet. "I was in the crapper. I only left him alone for a minute. The attendant went home sick an hour ago. I didn't even get the goddamn license number," his shrill trailed off. He turned, lunged inside.

I ditched. Othello and I slipped pine. Dashed. Stashed Davy Crocket, woolies, Fedora, in a blackberry thicket. Othello stuffed the coonskin into his jeans. We circled back to a hill above Louisiana Ave. overlooking Texaco. Torched smokes. Uncoiled, quaked, shuffled like prizefighters warming up for a ham-and-egger. Sat under dead trees. Twenty minutes withered. Texaco swarmed with federal agents on iguanas—waving moonbeams, hard-ons. Local bluebirds moped, sucking joe, cigs. Socrates sulked in circles, hands on his head. A frump in a housecoat clawed at his shoulders.

"Memphis's on a slab by now," Othello said softly. "The raven. You called it."

"He was primed to blow. It wasn't all our—"

"Shit." He dragged emphysema, looked down the hill. "She didn't have the ovaries to plan it, or did she?"

I laughed. Then Memphis Kane shoved a gas rag down my gullet. "Could have. Desperation's a funny bug."

"I'd fuck her either way."

"Crime of opportunity? À la Al Capone? Prohibition had presented so many felonious entrepreneurships that a man would've tripped over ten of them just schlepping to work."

"Kid on the dash, her kid, is dead. You get that?"

"No shit," I sarked.

"Know how many Blue Monkeys listened to the show?"

I shrugged.

"All sixty-seven."

The Cobra slipped back into the Texaco. We pricked. It stopped at the gas cocks. A skinny badge waved, yelled. Socrates and Housecoat froze, hugged. Ten bluebirds, flamethrowers set on flambé, crept toward Cobra. The door whined. Venus got out, pointed inside the car. Two birds planted her face-down, cuffed her. She played dead. A fed pried the passenger door, stuck his beak in, came out a winner. The cops cheered. So did we. Socrates steamed over. The fed handed him the brat. Venus stuffed into a maraschino cherry. It rolled into the night. Texaco died in five.

"We better crack this wishbone," I said. "I'll take 3. You take Red Beans and Rice to 5."

"We burlesque Siamese no matter what."

"Five's better."

We drifted Louisiana a workhouse blow job. Macked Suzy Qs. Quarter Pounders. Flashed thumbs. Ossified. A shit truck finally scooped us. We got lucky. Roto-Rooter was headed west on County Road 5. I made it home by two. Drowned in bathtub. SOS unanswered. Tuned my antenna to Raquel Welch. Came. Sat in my window. Torched an Old Gold. Othello's melancholic voice echoed in my head, *All sixty-seven.*

I slept in a cement mixer. Ch! Ch! Bam! Loop. Awoke at four. Was I a secondhand killer? Blue Monkeys gathered. Revenge got loaded at happy hour. I'd be the victim of a rape-murder. Get tumors. Tremors. Trichotillomania—Pop rushing me helter-skelter to the Mayo. S&M nurses! Straitjackets! Injections! Mused about Othello. Only one I could count on. Vowed to be his friend for life. *We burlesque Siamese no matter what.* I floated onto a Casablanca blossom, dozed.

Post Toasties. Kane's fish fry made *Saint Paul Dispatch's* page three. Bloated article, bio, photos, the whole bit. One line spooked me: Undisclosed sources claim Kane set himself on fire while giving an interview on a pirate radio station called Radio Dada.

I phoned Othello. "*Que pasa?*"

"Signing my will." A pause. "I saw it," he said.

"Saturday we'll do the gig. Apologize. Wave the olive branch to the Blue Monkeys."

"We killed Pancho Villa." Othello exhaled zephyr, paused. "I know. I know. We hopped a runaway train at the end of the tracks. Our fucked luck." He hung up.

I rang Zobar and Icee. They swore to keep zipped. Sure.

Radio Dada. Saturday. Seven trumpets. Lakewood Cemetery, downtown MPLS. Set up the ham in a gravedigger's shack we'd used before. Burned a Bubonic. Drained a half pint of

Rebel Yell.

Othello stoked a Hav-A-Tampa, vapored, "Radio Dada. From Earth. Time travelers who got off in the wrong century. This broadcast dedicated to the memory of one of our heroes, Gerald "Memphis" Kane. We regret and apologize for the events that led to Mr. Kane's taking of his own life on our show last week. We are at fault. We should have been more vigilant, should have seen the signs."

He syruped for a box of Kleenex. Finally, "This is Radio Dada's coda. Peace."

3

Year of the Manslaughterers passed. No FCC badges. No Blue Monkeys. I smelled burning flesh. Dead ravens. Pedophilic sex. Memphis Kane rioted in my dreams. Saw his face in the toilet. Convertibles. Sheri Duda's vagina. Possibility of the Blue Monkeys getting even made my black secret blister—D—depression. It'd had me by the throat since Santa Claus. It arrived even before I started jerking off to Miss December. Every day a bad audition. Flubbing my lines. Pay-phone stammer. Tripping over sweat. First-date shits. Insomnia. Anxiety golf-shoed my back, even with Marx Brothers on three a.m. TV.

Mowed lawns and shoveled snow to pay Panama Red for dime bags of tranquility. Clutching at solitaire's cold knees. Begging for sunstroke. For death. A new season. I made pretty masks. One for every game show—church—school—dating. Passion eluded me—waved like a prom queen from a frosty float. I was screwed into bedrock. Hips all tight. Teachers, classmates, parents mistook D for Devil-may-care. Some kids lauded my recklessness—girls especially. I cut class. Got drunk/stoned at lunch, before playing in football and hockey games. Wore my shitty grades like a medallion. Truth was, sometimes I hoped the Blue Monkeys, anybody, would cut my throat.

Then lava came rolling across the antenna plain. My girl! The road! She saved me! She fucked every guy in Jericho to get a shovel crew for my homecoming! They dug me out, and she set me on fire! Rolled me in Portland cement! I came up jangling Huckleberry.

Othello and I remained Siamese, hitching to elixir raffles, angels' houses; rambled Spiders from Mars. Othello had grown wise about D. We never jawed about it. Maybe he'd flashed how his dad was before his suicide.

"Mike's going to slay the motherfucking blues," he sang (as if I weren't there) during one of my wallows.

His words jumped my neurons. Crap spit out. Shame. Pork chops. Choir of cynics. Fat-legged women crawled in—flowery dresses—genteel—rubbed down my rusty coil with 3-in-One oil. Othello. My Scout! Befriended me for what I was.

4

Two years had Jiffy Popped since Memphis Kane's 11-45. Blue Monkeys remained Casper. My fear concerning retribution waned. Guilt over Kane's suicide? Lightening. Othello? Ha! He'd been swilling waters of Lethe. D looped. The tippytoe mauler. Swoop! Poof! I rumbled. Bloodied. Dizzy. Bastard loitered. Weeks. Months. I submerged D in Proust. Vodka. Masturbation. My perception?—Day: Fellini's cinematographer. Night: Nixon's proctologist. Sometimes I Spidered from Mars solo. Daring the wolves. They were busy licking their balls, tearing apart Jimmy Carter. D made me ashamed. Anemic. At times too spooked to hitch. I smooched isolation. Self-loathing. My Lenny Bruce doll. D also made me gutsy. Phlegmatic. Terminal. I scratched in notebooks. Neurotica. Exotica. Uranium recipes. Heroes sketched in margins: Cochise. Albert Hofmann. Nikola Tesla. I quit writing six months in. Switched to gin. Solzhenitsyn. It was shit anyway— matinee grunts—three-foot screams. I lusted for lucidity. Greek catapults. Western roads.

Pop knew all. Saw all. Wise to my hitching county roads. Laid down the law: Smooching highways—forbidden! Dublin dues! Bread and water for a week! Flagellations! Amputations! Highway 12 broke my cherry—murdered D! Bowie show in Pig's Eye/St. Paul. Seventy-five-mile merry-go-round. Six bells on Ziggy's night. I sported a Superman cape. Cap guns. Othello zipped his favorite looky-looky. Set his coonskin atop his black locks. Yellow neckerchief. Blue Union Army shirt, sergeant stripes. Dungarees tucked into calf-high moccasins. His trusty Buck knife hidden in an Indian. We slopped Blizzards at the Glen Lake DQ. Humped a shorty to the bigs—Highway 12 East. FDR's cum shot! We flashed thumbs. Crowed like roosters. Cars rocketed past. Two Old Golds. Nothing. Half a Bub's Daddy. Nothing! Othello's mercury dropped.

"We need something," he cracked.

"Breasts."

We laughed.

A '69 Shelby shellacked lemon meringue kicked gravel on the shoulder. Our getaway! Passenger door cried. Jammed noses inside. Creature from the Black Lagoon! A colossus! A trophy muskie! Welder's goggles. Greasy black bandana wrapped tightly around his head. Casey Jones overalls.

"Downtown Minneapolis," Blackie gurgled.

We plunged into the back seat—seaweed vinyl womb! Blackie reeked of hot waffles and bong water, but there was no bubbling on the way to Mill City. Chain sawed Marlboros. Tapped his fingers on the dash to Gene Vincent. Othello smirked wise, cocky—radiating Johnny rockets. My bronco kicked. Blackie dropped us at the Hennepin exit. Seventeen prostitutes flickered in a shit breeze. We hit up a Vietnamese street vendor. Shrunken heads, little American flags flapped atop his aluminum cart. Waited a pork pie, a Schlitz tall boy before a raven Caddy swooped in. A churchy car. Flashy as nun panties. We jumped in. A corncob preacher. Thump! Thump! Automatic door locks! We flew up the ramp. Cob glared into the rearview.

"You fellows are inviting sin dressed up in those ostentatious outfits," he scolded.

"So are you," syruped Othello.

"Ain't Superman a Christian?" I smacked.

He groaned, hiccupped a fuzz ball of acolyte pubic hair.

Othello slapped his sergeant stripes. "And what you got against the U.S. military, mister?"

Cob gazed to heaven for guidance. We nudged each other. Giggled. Cob kept his trap shut for a while. Gathered his angels. Then he firebolted the Bible the whole goddamned rest of the way to Pig's Eye. Jesus this, Jesus that! St. Paul via Matthew, Mark, Luke, and John—we were blistered as black sheep on Judgment Day by the time we got there.

Bowie gassed Chinese! Crooned caramel! Mugged Iggy Pop! Post-gig, we floated Kellogg toward 12. Mercurial! Anointed! Hashed Venus! Othello waved his prize—jade's number scrawled on his palm with Bic. He fanned his coonskin. Genuflected. Milked his balls.

"I got to second during 'Suffragette City,'" he boasted. "The little twist in the yellow halter!" He winked. "Christ, how about you? The cake nursing you could've converted St. Paul to atheism."

I shrugged. "Said she has a boyfriend or some crap."

Pig's Eye's granite monoliths loomed under July's hot flame. Eerie as a pioneer graveyard. Gazed down at the riverbank. The Mississippi belched. Coughed up Sioux. Huck Finn and Jim floated by on a raft.

Scout eyeballed me. "What?" he asked.

"I'm going Gene Autry for good!"

Scout raised his eyebrows. Donned a look of skepticism. "You sure this time? California ain't no cowboy movie."

"Thanks, Papa. My social security card came in the mail. Legal to work now."

"Still think you'll get hired at some ranch? At sixteen?"

"Sure! You got to—"

"I know. I know. Throw yourself out there. And a good man will land somewhere. Might even strike pay dirt."

"You're catching on, boy." Threw my hands up. "I need a place where the goddamn state pastime is something other than gossiping. Land O' Lakes bumpkins! It's Route 66 for me, bub."

"The west is the best," Othello sang, imitating Jim Morrison. "And the old man?"

"Might as well put a mountain range between him and me. Hell, even the Rockies might not be enough."

"And how!" he chuckled with a hint of fear. "Didn't you tell me once you had relatives in New York?"

"Too freezo. Haven't seen them in years. We left when I was four."

I lit a smoke. Looked off at the gurgler. Othello studied my eyes. Fidgeted. Tenderly slapped my shoulder twice. Knew he worried about me going off alone. The thought scared me to death. But I had to bust out!

"You should cut, too. Stay here too long, you'll never get out."

His eyes bore into mine. "I'm not ready, Mike," he said softly. Knew he worried about leaving Flo alone.

We'd regained our swagger by the time we reached the bottom of 12's chute. Unconquered! Swollen! Cheeky as Charlie! Othello twirled his coon tail. I blew Old Gold smoke. A copper '59 Impala wiggled its tail fins at us. Squealed on the shoulder. Bumper sticker read "Proud to be Polish." We ran up to the convertible's passenger door. A Zuhrah Shriner tapped his red fez.

"Late for tadpoles to be floating on the pond, ain't it?" he bellowed in a Nordeast Minneapolis monotone.

We warily eyed our prize. He looked old. At least thirty. Reedy. Bulldog face. Dense as a can of Spam.

"Peter Lorre needs his eyes back," I cracked and thought about waving the loser on.

He snorted. "And Superman needs his cape back," he japed. Reached into his white dress-shirt pocket. Flicked a Camel. Sparked a Zippo. "You know, a gol darn loon might come along and gobble a tadpole up."

"A loon fudging a little Shriner's hat?" Othello sassed, raising his pitch an octave.

Shriner dodged it, faked a smile. He plucked a deep-fried mosquito off the dash—big as a stork! He belched, took a mammoth bite.

"The dash," I whispered.

"A Polack's shrine," laughed Scout.

Don Ho bobble head. Half a bratwurst. Baby Ruth wrappers. Archie comics. Can of mackerel. Naked hula-girl dolls.

"Care for some debauchery?" Shriner asked with a grin and a wink.

"Pedophiliac?" I razored.

"Heck, no!" he howled. "Naked waitresses!"

"Where?" asked Othello.

"Milo's X-Ray. Cedar and East Fourth. Lowertown. Near the river. The vixens at Milo's will make your wiener swell up to the size of a can of corn."

We laughed. We slid into the back seat. I smelled bug spray. BO. A pile of rotting dreams.

Fez wolfed the rest of the buzz-buzz, burped, and swiveled. "Catch the show at the Civic Center, eh?"

"Uh-huh," we said in unison.

"You know, Bowie has some real nice songs, then," he said, shifted into drive, and eased back toward the Civic Center. "But a guy has trouble liking an oddball, you know."

We chuckled at the fool.

"I'm Bernie," he said. "Mother named me after Bernard of Menthon," he whispered, his voice breaking.

"Who?" I asked without giving a shit.

"A heroic monk. They named the St. Bernard dog after him," he mumbled with a peanut of pride. "What do you tadpoles go by?"

"Spanky and Alfalfa," I said.

Shriner sniffled. "Well Little Rascals, they won't card you at Milo's." He flipped open the glove. Yanked out a pint of Snowshoe Grog—half bourbon, half peppermint schnapps. Tipped it. Passed it.

"Why's that?" I asked. Took a short pull, handed it to Scout.

"I used to run with Billy Bright, the head bouncer." He torched another hump. "Yah know, there's leftover hot dish back there," he crowed. "Tuna marshmallow Milk Duds."

We winced. Scout lifted the *Minneapolis Tribune* obituary page off the floorboards and there it was. A CorningWare of

Minnesota hot dish! Fuming smegma! Served at hangings! Disembowelments! Lutheran weddings!

"Ever seen naked girlies?" hit Shriner.

"Fingerbanged Darla Hood's pussy once," I snotted, trying to conceal my excitement. Had never been to a strip club before. Imagined Milo's centerfolds! Older women! Bouncing! Strutting!

"You guys finish that Snowshoe off," he said, waved his hand, hung a Louie on Fort Road. "Been higher than Paul Bunyan since I nigger-lipped a J of Kona at Nye's happy hour!"

Othello's glare melted the rearview. Shriner caught his eye.

"Had a super-duper polka band over there," he chirped, unafraid.

A Hmong driver swerved. Breezed our radiator. Shriner smoked the brakes.

"Hoser!" he shouted. He patted his fez. "Jeez! What's with the goddamned slopes? It's a jackass screw job the way they let these foreigners have the run of—"

"What in hell do Shriners do besides screw chimps at circuses?" Othello horned in.

Bernie ignored the jab. "I get more beaver wearing this fez than Ted Nugent with his boner pants and suspenders."

"Blow-up beav," I said.

"We're mysterious as Eskimos in Egypt," he smirked. Tapped his fez. "Gives gals a hard-on." He swung right on Jackson.

"How do you sign up?" Othello blipped sarcastically.

"Well, you Rascals look white enough, but the Nobles would want to dig up your ancestors' bones back to the Civil War. Make sure you're all chalk."

"Pull over!" I howled, eyeing Scout.

Othello drew an index finger across his throat.

"Sorry. Jeez. That's just how it is: the Zuhrah doesn't take jigaboos, fish heads, or tack-ohs."

Othello balled his fists.

"Used to be a guy could come downtown with no worries. Now, a guy comes downtown, and all he sees is niggers! Niggers! Niggers! Niggers!"

"Jesus fucking Christ!" screamed Othello.

Bernie sucked in his cheeks. Made bug eyes feigning shock. "Weeeeeeel!" he hollered mockingly and laughed, "Everyone's racist! You bambinos, too."

I leaned toward Scout and cooed singsong, "Naked waitresses. We'll ditch this asshole once we get inside."

He nodded, pulled the Buck from his Indian. Found Impala's liver! Quietly carved a circle big as a bull's-eye on the back of Bernie's seat. "KKK" in its center. I nodded in approval. Ten minutes oozed.

Blue neon sign blinked "Milo's X-Ray." Shriner glided into the parking lot. Muscle cars. Porky Buicks. Dead Puritans.

"In case Billy Bright ain't at the door, we need to bury your rosebuds!" he said. "Pass me that Snowshoe." I complied. He splashed grog onto his palm. Rubbed it on his cheeks. Passed back to me. We swigged—only pretended to use it as aftershave. Bernie jerked out Wildroot hair tonic from the glove. Flaunted it like a snake-oil huckster. We rolled our eyes. "This and stogies drive the ladies nutso!" he beamed. "Know what else?" he asked coyly. "Up north, this is Chippewa mouthwash!" and he began to giggle uncontrollably, his bulldog mug becoming hideous—frenetic. He peeled off his fez. Lovingly propped it on his lap. Shook out globs of Wildroot and massaged his scalp. Passed it. We aped.

"Any spare fezzes we can wear?" I asked. "You know, just for fun?"

"Jesus, mother of Arabs!" Bernie blurted indignantly. "If the Divan—or worse—if the Potentate found out, I'd get defezzed!" Patted his fez protectively. Stuck a J—Kona Gold, I hoped—between his canines. Flamed Zippo. Passed bhang.

"My mother died this morning," he said casually.

"What?" I asked.

He went mute. Tickled his fez's tassel.

"She's in the trunk," he finally said.

"What?!" I shrieked.

Othello banged the door open. Motioned to skedaddle. We sprang out.

"I killed her," he called after us. "Please don't go! I only did it because she asked me to!"

"Why?" shot Othello. "Why would she—"

"Lou Gehrig's disease. Doc only gave her six—"

"Why did you put her in the trunk?" I asked. "Why didn't you call an ambulance, the bluebirds?"

"No one'll understand!" he wailed. "I'm too goddamned cute to go to the hoosegow!"

He followed us out. Paced. A minute dripped.

"I've been too gummed up about it," he said matter-of-factly. "I'm going nutso with grief. But later I'll go to the police station."

Scout and I looked at each other. We silently agreed Bernie had a credibility problem.

"I need a highball and lickety-split," Shriner said.

"Let's see the body," I demanded.

"Oh, heck no!" he shrieked. "Jeez! No fricking way!"

"Come on!" I begged, calling his bluff. But Othello looked at me with pleading eyes. Shook his head no. Backed away from the car. Shit! The weed and booze made me forget Scout'd discovered his dad's dead body.

Bernie eyed Scout. Lurched in circles. Threw up his hands. Glared at me. "He's right, you know," he said. "You tadpoles are too gol darn young for such business."

I stared him down, and his carousel braked. "The trunk latch busted," he muttered. "It's tied down with twine."

Othello crept toward me. Eyed me for a long moment. Reluctantly pulled his Buck. Tossed it to me. Took three giant steps backward. I unsheathed Buck. Slapped it into Bernie's palm.

"Okay, but you can't touch her, then. You have to stay back."

Bernie snailed. Met me at the Impala's bloody ass. Bent down over the trunk. Othello hung back. Shook his arms and legs like a sprinter about to drop into starter blocks.

Bernie fumbled the knife, the twine. Trunk popped! Hissing Sicilian clam! Organ music! Fog! Courtesy light blazed. His knife-holding silhouette a bugaboo!

Bernie peeled back the camouflage tarp. Looked away. I gaped! Gulped! The goblin lay face-up. Sixty winters. Ratty pink housecoat. Ajax hands. Hair a pouf of orange cotton candy. Forehead and face bloody as a Washburn steak. Mouth suspended in a comical scream—a putrid green flood gushing out!—filled with foreclosure notices—psychiatrists—empty bottles of gin—rabbis. Pluck! Pluck! Hmmm! A cello. Playing an entrancing Polish aria—peaceful as light mist falling in the pines. I stared—with awe!—with horror! But I couldn't take my eyes off her! I felt lewd! Pummeled by a rock-throwing mob! In violation!—like when I'd fondled a four-year-old neighbor girl when I was six. *But you can't touch her.* I did want to touch her—not there. Bernie hyperventilated—a hundred miles away—wheezing plastic monsters. Now I was part of this treachery! A fucking witness! An accessory?

He nudged me. Clumsily pulled tarp over the body. Cut new twine. Tied the trunk down as if the twine were on fire. Handed me the blade. I sheathed it, passed it back to Othello. He stood totem. He had the mumps.

"I told you, tadpole," Bernie snuffled.

He twirled, came at me, tentacles outstretched! They found me! Suck! Pop! Splop! His arms crunched my ribs, his octopus beak gaped. Woolly boys screamed for help!

"Why'd I listen to her?" he moaned. "Why? Why?"

"Because you're a dutiful son," I gasped.

"I'm following Mom!" he bleated. "Tonight!"

Othello ciphered behind Bernie's back that we should hightail. The Shriner finally cut the suction, and I reeled backward.

"I did it with a pipe wrench," Bernie said, sniveling snot. "She hated pills. Thought about rat poison, you know. Buckshot."

He let out a muffled cry, punked toward Milo's X-Ray. I checked Othello's willingness. Half a tank. I mimed tits. Othello shrugged, sighed. We followed on Bernie's heels. Billy Bright stood at the portal. Swank. Roman. Jubilee eyes. Scarred cheek. Drinking age eighteen. We looked fourteen. He ran eyes over Scout's Union Army duds, my Superman outfit, tilted his head back, and laughed.

"Check your six-shooters here," he said.

"Let him wear 'em," whined the Shriner. "They're only cap guns."

"Christ, I know that, you stupid Polack," snarled Billy Bright, and he cracked his knuckles menacingly. "Last Halloween we let a guy in with fake pistols. Stuck a barrel up a waitress's glory hole. Fucking boyfriend tried to torch the place a week later." I unbuckled my gun belt. Handed the rig over. Billy Bright tossed it on his chair. Clanked sword. Frisked. Felt up the Buck in Othello's Indian. Othello forfeited. Shooed us into a blighted foyer reeking of sex. Puke. Nevada Gas. A blown-up, backlit chest x-ray on the wall. Snowball tumor! "Milo Horn's X-Ray" scripted underneath! Three tricked-out cig machines blinked against the wall.

"What are these?" asked Othello.

"Aura machines," said Bernie. "Larry, Moe, and Curly. From some Nazi death camp. Using dope as weapons. Nazi LSD."

"Bullshit," I said.

"It's true, or I'm a Heeb's uncle. It was one of Josef Mengele's experiments. You know, the Angel of Death bastard that performed all sorts of wicked-ass experiments on children. Tried it out on a bunch of captured nigger flyboys. Some went completely nutso. Some went suicide. But that was after doping them up ten times a day for a fricking month. The Stooges will only give you a little zing."

Othello frowned again, raised an eyebrow. "Nigger flyboys, huh? You tried it?"

"You betcha!"

"And?"

The Shriner's face split into a wide grin. "An hour of euphoria."

Othello and I looked at each other. Why not? We'd dropped Purple Haze twice the previous year. I figured the Shriner's Nazi tale was mostly a stretcher. Slid sawbuck in Curly. Eyed Delirium Number 13. Scout cackled. Pulled lever. We pressed eyes to the zygote orifice. Hum! Rattle! Two bright flashes! We staggered. Numb. Yellow fits. Calm. Eyes adjusted.

Shriner pushed through operating-room doors. Moans. Screeches. Lou Reed's "Perfect Day" rained warm ash. Mirrored floor. Bright red walls. More x-rays. Fractured femurs. Crushed skulls. Dozen lime-green 1950s x-ray tables scattered. Booby hatch beds—restraints, headgear. Gods, monsters—sipping sulfuric. Swapping lies. Chemical bath burbled with hepcats. Indians. Tuna surgeons. Naked waitresses weaved. Covered in talcum powder. Handprints. Hot, as promised! Shriner perched at an operating table on the back wall. We bellied. He smiled. Two Swedes with Goodyear tits, sheared snatches pirouetted. Our eyes bugged Panavision.

"Pros," said Shriner. "Cost plenty of coin."

Bartender welled up. Broad. Butch. Face a bucket of bullheads. "Humans Suck" T-shirt. Bazooka Joe perfume. Polar stare.

"What'll ya have, then?"

"A Black President," said Bernie. Popped a Camel. Flamed his Zippo.

"Suds?" asked Othello.

"Grain Belt, Schmidt, Leinenkugel." She raked her crew cut.

"Michelob?" I asked. "Miller?"

"No foreign beer."

Bernie guffawed. Wiped a tear.

"Grain Belt," I said.

"Me, too," said Othello.

As she waddled off, Bernie called out, "Say there, darling!"

Bazooka turned back, yawned. Hands on hips. Forced a smile.

"A round of deep-fried Twinkies on a stick!"

"Chocolate dipped?"

"You betcha!"

Othello and I watched the Swedes fish-juice a swarm of Sioux iron workers. Bazooka slid a Jagermeister-Coke under Bernie's veil. He guzzled half. A queer Groucho Marx drizzled. Shirtless. In a G-string. Wagged his Pat Boone tattoo at Othello. Moved in. Scout snapped his G-string. Groucho threw a right. Knocked him off his stool, and the joint erupted in laughter. Othello rose with phony panache. Hoots! Catcalls! Greasy fists jackhammered the bar. Groucho bowed. Drifted away. Bazooka slid us our beers. Twinkies. Delirium Number 13 began to fade. I felt spongy. Anemic. Buddhist. I wolfed my Twinkie. Slammed the Grain Belt.

Bernie cupped his mitt over my ear. "I'm ready to piss on

Dick Tracy's loafers. Go to the cops with me tonight?"
I hesitated.

My guardian angel slugged me. Onioned, "Don't go! Shriner regrets his confession. He'll cut out your fucking eyes! Slice off your ears! Dump your bones in Catfish Cemetery!"

"Yeah, sure," I said to Bernie.

The Shriner flashed bleeding gums at me. Covered his face. Othello clutched my shoulder, mouthed, "Let's go."

"He says he wants us to go to the dicks with him," I whispered.

"No way!"

Ten minutes jittered. Bernie's eyes met mine. Jerked his head toward the bathroom and then shitbagged out.

"Come on!" Othello bossed and yanked me off the barstool. Billy Bright loomed. Feigned Betty Boop. Winked. Jerked dimples toward the back. We recouped our weapons, slipped like slithering fish past the kitchen. Down a murky coil. Freud on his knees! Giving head to a Moroccan boy. EXIT blinked! Othello cracked the door to the alley. Weaseled both ways.

"Dark as shit," he whispered.

We greased twenty yards. Then the Impala! Parked sideways. Blocking the alley. I heard a shell echo in the chamber of a pump shotgun. We spun around. Bernie wielded a Police Special. The barrels found us. Wide as Lowry Tunnel!

"Tadpoles think you're pretty—"

The Impala trunk creaked behind us. Bernie's mom flopped out! Rose rickety, clutching a pipe wrench. Stumbled toward us.

"He tried to kill me!" she screamed and careened past us toward Bernie waving the wrench like a tomahawk. "That crazy son of a bitch thinks he's my son and—!"

Othello zipped past Mom and lunged for Shriner. Kicked him in the balls. Bernie doubled over. Scout wrestled the thunder stick away. Grabbed the barrel, stepped back, and whacked Shriner's head three times like he was felling an oak. The sound! Blood splattered Mom's pink housecoat. Bernie crumb-caked. His dented fez landed at my feet. Zapruder film whirred! JFK's head blowing open. Jackie climbing onto the trunk. Othello stood over his foe—swinging the shotgun across his thighs with one hand. Chest heaving. His face—delirious!—primal! He was ready to crouch down! Tear canines into entrails! I walked to the hunter. He looked up. Eyeballed me as if I were a stranger—quarry—noting my defects! Smelling my fear! "You ignorant fuck!" screamed the woman. "It's all a joke!" She knelt over Humpty. Pulled off her red wig. Wavy silky black mane! Peeled off a thin latex mask exposing a pinup face! "What?!" I cried. Othello dropped the shotgun. Shrunk. Stepped back. The babe gently lifted Bernie's soft-boiled. Runny as the Redbird Special. She crammed her wig underneath it.

"I am an actor," Shriner wheezed in a blue-blood accent. "Moonlighting from the Guthrie. Genevieve, would you ask these young gentlemen to assist you in getting me to a hospital. I believe I'll require succor." He exited the stage, eyes fluttering.

"Fucking do something!" wailed the woman. "Help me get him to a hospital!"

"Gush first, or we're ditching," growled Othello.

Scout lifted Shakespeare's torso, cradled his head. Gently slapped his roses, trying to bring him around. More juice spattered Silky's coat. He untied his neckerchief. Used it to wrap the fool's crimson. Bernie entered stage left. Silky sighed.

"I'm fine. I'll be fine, dear," he said and scrunched up his mug in pain. "Oh, but I do think I should linger here a bit longer until my faculties return."

"Howard's my boyfriend," she meowed. Pawed his brow. "We're method actors, like Brando. We have to live the part. We solicit the Civic Center after shows for a fresh audience."

"Congratu-fucking-lations," I said.

"Check the gun," she sneered. "They're blanks."

I scooped up the rocket. Cracked it open and saw the funny bullets.

"We never know what the Devil's going to unfold," she giggled. "That's the thrill of it! Some run. Some cry. Some throw up. But this—"

"You take chances," mumbled Othello as he repeatedly tugged on the tail of his coonskin—scared out of his mind.

"Some son bitch with a gun, or a *knife*, might cancel your act. Never rehearsed that, huh?"

"We only pick up easy marks like you to fill the role of the deuteragonist, don't we Genie?" Howard said. "Oh, it's nothing personal, lads, please understand."

"It'll be okay, honey," Genie mewed. She bared her fangs at us. "You boys need to take some responsibility for what happened here, too."

"Responsibility!?" snapped Othello. "For protecting ourselves from some freak with a twelve-gauge? Fuck that, lady! We're only sixteen! What you got, huh? Some lame con you play out on kids? With a fucking wig and a skull cap?"

Genie shrank.

Howard rolled, propped himself up on one elbow. He jutted out his Machiavellian chin and glared at me. "Well, after all, you were quite eager and enthusiastic to see a 'corpse,' weren't you?" he puffed. "Hmm?"

"Who ain't?" I cracked. My eyes darted to Othello. He looked away.

Genie smirked. "Less than half stay around after Howard informs them that he's killed his mother and deposited her corpse in his trunk."

"And more than half of those who stay manage to escape before we get to the alley scene," said Howard.

"Shriner getup?" I asked.

"A friend's uncle," Genie chirped. She goo-gooed at her beau. "Howard's played a Rabbi, a bisexual farmer, a Culligan man, a proctologist. And I think his Shriner is just as convincing, don't you?"

"Only with you as my leading lady," Howard whispered. Then he cancelled the burlesque. Floated Dante.

"Howard! Howard!" Genie screeched. She shook him like a busted radio. His eyes rolled white.

I checked the jumper in his neck. Zzzz! Dead! No! But he said he was okay! Why didn't we shut up and take him to the hospital like he wanted? His ghost! It was going to dog us! Othello stood up. Backed away.

"Howard!" Genie sobbed. "Come on!"

Her wild eyes darted between me and Othello—measuring for a police sketch artist? Coffins? She jumped onto her haunches, clenched both fists, looking ready to dash to Winnipeg! She bolted for the Impala. Othello tackled her. Threw her in the trunk. Slammed it shut.

Genie screamed. Pounded.

"Come on!" Othello brayed, and he tore down the alley without looking back.

"Othello!" I cried out. "Wait! Othello!" I raced ten yards after his shrinking silhouette and stopped. Ripped off my Superman cape. Stuffed it into my Levi's. Hustled back to the Impala. Crept up to the trunk like a phantom.

"Let's hear your song, Genie," I called out.

"What?"

"What you going to tell the coppers?"

"I've thought about that! We were besieged by Negroes! And, oh! Poor Howard!" She hesitated for a long while. "Neither you nor I committed a crime."

"There's blood on your hands, just the same."

Silence.

"I'm taking the shotgun and the blanks. If you sick the cops on us, we'll have proof of your and Howard's con. They'll take a bite out of you one way or another. If you keep mum, we'll keep mum."

I retrieved the keys from the ignition. Dashed to Howard's corpse. Scooped up the rocket. Scenes bled of Genie falling prey to sodomites—killers. Ran back to the Impala. Diddled its rump. The lock wasn't broken. Popped the coffin. Genie scratched out looking deader than the first time I'd seen her. I tore down the alley following Othello's tracks.

Had to stash my pal's jail ticket. But where? The river? They might drag the old man. Where was Pop when I needed him! He'd shove it up my ass—lock, stock, and barrel! Jetted toward the Mississippi. Past tarantulas! Parole officers! Giant priests! Fifty yards. An abandoned slaughterhouse beckoned. Dark doorways! Found one. Ducked into shadows. Smelled blood.

Rat brains. The Impala crawled past! Waited half an hour.
Waltzed down another alley like Sunday afternoon. No sign of
Othello. That's when Lady Luck sprinkled stardust! Horse piss!
A flower-shop Dumpster! Reached in. Yanked out a long-
stemmed-roses box. Fred Astaired the rocket. Shoved it inside.
Tossed my Superman cape into the bin. Ambled a mile along
the Mississippi. Figured the cops wouldn't drag it that far. Just
a beau on a social call! A ham on rye. Swiveled for Genie. Dicks.
Made Shepard Road's laced-curtain castles. Continued along
the gurgler. Took a shit on the mayor's side lawn. Walked another half mile. Wiped the flamer down with my shirt. Flung it
into a snarl of dead wood along with the last roses of my youth.
They sank. I exhaled! Erupted in tears. Donned lizard skin. Tiptoed Mayberry streets east toward 35E.

Thumbed 12's West ramp. A black nurse rumbled cinders
in a rusty LTD. She pulled graves at Methodist Hospital. Big
laugh. Andouille legs busted out of support hose. Told "white"
jokes—hilarious as a phony Shriner getting his brains bashed
in. Nursie dumped me on another sour punch line, County
Road 3, close to home. A milk truck curdled—a burly Kraut
farm boy chomping Red Man. I sat on the hup-two step. Vincent Price slid in next to me. Slung his arm around my shoulder. Blew a smoke ring.

"Congratulations, my boy," he said. "I'll never forget my first
murder. The screams. The blood." He searched my expression-
less face. "It was murder tonight, you know. Premeditated! Such
a feat for one so young! Oh, yes! Othello began hatching his
evil plot when the deceased took a left on 'Niggers, Niggers,
Niggers.' A knife across the gizzard. Easy-peasy. But fate served
up the poor boob on a platter of kielbasa and fried onions. And
you my boy, are an accessory for ditching the murder weapon.
Thinking about saving your skin, aren't you? Telling your father? The authorities? Think hard. There's a killer on the loose."
Vincent evanesced.

Farm boy chucked me a furlong from home. It was four a.m.
I hobbled up Westmill Road. Made a run for it. Armed with a
string of fresh lies—the eloquent last words of a dead man!

Crammed with cowardice, I split in half. Slid under the door. Pop didn't hear me come in.

Insomnia jabbered. D plucked my ribs. Stuck its filthy finger up my ass. I moped into the kitchen at six. Slopped black coffee—funny bullets smothered in Pepto-Bismol—a side of live hornets.

5

Buzzed Othello's Corn Flakes.

"Virgin patrol!" Flo cackled into the receiver, already drunk.

"How you doing, Mrs. Bolen?"

"Better than you, pubescent," she slurred, dropped the phone. Silence. Panting.

"Track star," I said.

No answer.

"Got your blue ribbon."

"Forfeited," Othello whispered.

"What are you—?"

"Slitting my wrists."

I swallowed an arrest warrant. "I went back for the gun. Ditched Genie, wiped the prints, threw it in the Mississippi far past the dragline."

"I burned my coonskin and my army duds," he muttered sadly. "Check the funnies?"

"Old Mick has it in the crapper."

"It's on page six."

"Fuck!"

"No mention of us."

"Read it to me!"

"'The body of a thirty-one-year-old Minneapolis man, Howard Strum, an apparent victim of murder, was found in St. Paul early this morning by St. Paul police after receiving an anonymous tip. Strum had been a popular actor at the Guthrie Theater for the past three years. St. Paul police are asking for any witnesses to step forward. A reward has been offered.'"

I exhaled confetti. "Genie the balladeer! The coppers don't have anything concrete they can pin on us, anyway."

"Don't they?"

"What?"

"You bawled out my name two or three times when I ran off. Remember?"

"Shit! I did! I'm sorry. Maybe she didn't hear it clearly."

"Maybe she did. How many high school kids in the Twin Cities with my name? Hell, all the cops got to do is get on the horn to all the schools and match my name up against their rosters. My coonskin will be a dead giveaway."

"Only if Genie actually did hear your name, and only if she decides to squeal."

"What about his pal Billy Bright? And the bartender and the wigglers and half the assholes in Milo's X-Ray?"

"Only Genie saw the last act."

"And—and—and you!"

"Me? I'm in the shit, too, you know!" I shut up. Sucked star dust. "Let's hope Genie twirled the cops. And if she didn't give your name up, then we can infer she didn't give it to Billy Bright or anyone else, either."

"Infer? You sound like—like—like the—the DA."

"You sound like Elmer Fudd after a Black Beauty suppository."

"We can infer—we—I'm still in hot water!" he moaned. He paused, whispered, "I miss my Dad."

A long silence.

"Scout?"

"Tonight, midnight. Meet me at old Radio Dada on Purgatory, alone." He hung up.

Mom and Pop went to bed at eleven. I stole two cans of Pabst and slipped out at half past. Scout's tone on the horn had made me waxen. Jittery. Cold as a workhouse bunk. I bugged along Purgatory. Our band resumed hanging at the main Radio Dada site a year ago. Bluebirds had stripped the place after Memphis Kane's suicide. We'd since refurbished, but there'd been no broadcasts since Othello's apology to the Blue Monkeys.

Called out, "Man Ray," as I approached. Othello volleyed.

I slipped into the Visqueen cunt, side-stepping empty wine and beer bottles. Lava lamps glowed in back. Ten strides took me to Othello—strapped in an electric chair. He flicked a cigarette, gazed up, and grinned Dillinger. I deflated. Dropped into the witness stand. Eyed the fresh pile of *Furry Freak Brothers* comics and *Playboy*. Cracked a beer. Handed Scout the other.

"Exactly how did you leave Genie?" he rocketed.

"I let her out of the trunk right before I took off. Didn't want to leave her to the wolves."

He raised an eyebrow. "Uh-huh," he muttered with disappointment.

"What? Want her dead, too?"

He shrugged. Hit his beer. Took a gulp off a half pint of Jack. "I'm a murderer, Mike."

"It was self-defense, cut-and-dried." I ignored Vincent peering over Othello's shoulder.

My confederate's droopy, bloodshot eyes wrestled mine. "I killed a man just the same." He buried his face in his mitts. Muffled cries. Growls. "I wanted to kill the bigot in his car, in Milo's!"

"It was his fucking fault! I want to kill Pop once a week. Doesn't mean I'm ever going to do it."

Scout looked up.

"We'll keep mum. Low profile," I said.

"What am I going to tell people when they ask about my coonskin?"

"Tell them you grew out of it like Linus and his security blanket."

"He never outgrew it."

"Fuck Linus. Then say one of your girlfriends stole it."

He jumped up and smiled. His eyes blazing Fourth of July! He wrenched my arm. "You and me! A secret pact! Hush-hush! Like *Tom Sawyer*! How about it?"

Redundant! I wanted to blurt my secret promise to be his pal for life after Memphis Kane's suicide, but I kept quiet. He pulled his bolo. Slit palm. Handed me knife. Drilled my eyes. I gave in. Cut. We clasped knuckles.

Othello whispered, and I repeated each sentence, "We swear on this blood oath to keep mum about last night at any and all cost. Even upon threat of death or reform school. We also swear our heart-of-hearts pledge to be loyal and true to one another until both of us are dead."

His manic smile faded to black. "My Dad would know what to do," he said sorrowfully. "I'll never turn myself in! I'd rather be dead than do a stretch in the workhouse!" He rained. Wind. Hail. I hugged him. He wept harder. We killed Jack by one thirty. I got home at two.

6

The days seeped like a pustule! Like dead sperm! Fate taunted. I was threshed wheat. Locusts swarmed. Coming for me. Relentless. Rapacious! Breeching laser wire. Devouring my shrill prayers. Devouring shotguns. Dead actors. One month. Black. Two months. Blue. Badges crashed my dreams. D fucked me. Held me underwater. Fingered open my eyelids. Gave me cobalt injections.

The bluebirds found their boy six moons later. They dragged Othello at three a.m. to a Pig's Eye blab room. Screaming. Peter Pan underwear. Heart wrapped in duct tape. He wiggled in the Petri dish while the gumshoes poked him like seventh-grade boys dissecting a frog. Piss squirted in their faces. Flo was at the grilling. She played the ashen queen. Howard's skeleton jangled on her raunchy thighs.

I saw Othello two clocks later. He looked DOA. The cops claimed a witness said there were two of us, but Scout didn't rat me out, denied everything. Did Genie sing? Somebody from Milo's? Howard's shotgun burbled in my mind! We were fucked. Rumors made the school hit parade. Scenes of incarceration! Gang rapes! My fingers cut off with a jigsaw blade! Revelations floated. Bloated! Wormy as a week-old corpse! Lost more Zs. Bought a Bible. A gun. A cemetery plot. Othello bought track shoes. A month later, at sixteen, Othello Bolen disappeared. Flo dogged me. No word from him. No word from Jesus. I tossed the Gideon. Kids graped that Othello now farted with angels. Slung lightning in a Georgia revival. My gut said he'd headed west.

Three months later, I started slaving at a Standard station in Hopkins. A step up from mowing Lady of the Lake's lawn. Pumping gas—jerking dipsticks—kissing ass—Othello screwing my best girl, maybe even shoveling shit on the ranch I'd dreamed for myself. Considered joining him. Got cold feet. Confessed I wasn't ready, either. Finally as honest as my murdering friend. D, Pop squeezed me.

Right around then I got the call I'd dreaded.

"Mikey boy, the fuzz weaseled by here again yesterday," boozed Flo. "Thought you should know they asked about little old you."

"You didn't give them my name?!"

"Oh, Christ, no! I didn't tell them a teensy weensy thing, rube." I heard her gulp from her martini. "Did Othello kill that man?"

I ignored the dagger, shot, "Sure you didn't say my name?"

"I said Othello has a lot of friends. A damn popular kid!"

"Why now?"

"Sounds like they're cutting some kind of flowery goddamned plea with the girlfriend."

"The girlfriend?"

"Genevieve Something-or-other. Genie the strumpet. Genie the whore. My guess, they're squeezing her daddy's balls. Juicing his wallet. Probably finding god-awful screwy conflicting evidence in that hussy's yarn."

"Thanks, Mrs. Bolen," I whispered.

Deafening silence.

"Mike?"

"Uh-huh."

"Did Othello kill that man?"

Lightning! Sky split open. Whirlwinds! Sucking sounds! Shrieks!

"Mike. Did he?!"

"Sorry Mrs. Bolen. I can't. I—"

"Oh, Mike!" she whimpered. Slammed the horn down.

I ran outside. Flapped my kid wings. Caught six feet of air before crashing into Pop's electric fence. Trailed tears back into the house. Ate liver and onions. Barfed to Rochester.

7

A year bled out, and the bluebirds never crapped on my wire! A postcard came: a color flick of a handsome silver-haired man cradling a bomb. Caption read "Atomic Al's Nuclear Supply." Flipped it over. Blank! Othello! Postmarked Los Alamos, NM. I shoved it into *Hustler*. I didn't bleep. Not even to Flo. Guilt panged for not telling her.

Arm & Hammer flung me a cap and gown. "He'll never make it!" printed on it. Pumped gas at Ice Station Hilda, continued to mooch at home. Miserly, saving for my escape. First I would find Othello. And then—flipped a coin between San Diego, Key West—as far away from Pop as possible. Tails! San Diego! I was bent on finding Othello along the way. Bought a '66 Mustang at the South St. Paul Stockyard's novena lot. Caballo was moonblind. With bowed tendons. Cracked hooves.

Pop gathered a galloglass brigade to scrap my exodus. War trumpets! Long swords! Foamy wolfhounds! They encamped at the bottom of the hill on Westmill Road. Bonfire. Roasted deer and the nosy neighbor lady. The old man shaved his head for battle. Set wicked traps. Banged drums! His fists stalked me. I whirled home one Friday. Dead drunk. Ripe for mutiny! Lions! Reeking from a bleach's sweaty pussy at Lucky U Motel.

Pop, robed in Irish Mist, bubbled from his cathedra. "You won't last out in California three Sabbaths, friend!" He spewed hot ash. "No pluck. Hell, you damn near flunked high school!"

"You've damn near flunked fatherhood."

"When you running off?" he spit back.

"The ides of March."

"*Et tu, Brute?*"

"*Et ego.*"

"Someday, you too, will know the curse of power," he whispered forlornly, and then he reared up and hurled, "Wherever you go, there I'll be!"

Arrows found me! I put another rock in my sling. "You've lost your Everlast heavy bag. Who you going to knock around when I'm gone? I'm the only knucklehead who'll take it! The other kids have brains. You'll miss me."

He waved like shooing a fly, taunted, "Been at a goddamn pot party since you were thirteen. You call crying, and I'll think about sending a bus ticket to whatever damn town you chicken out in."

"I'll put in a good word for you at the booby hatch."

Pop turned his V-stare to high. Ascended the stairs with a wake of chimps, the brownies caressing his heels.

He and I bloodied a month. Howard Strum's skull in my pocket. Lightning overhead. My mind a scorched field where D's ravens fed. Howard's death scene flickered daily. Fucker deserved it! Pop boiled tumors and carrots. Shot the neighbor's dog. Father Glinka, our church's pastor, fluttered in with a gallon of holy water. Pop's bullwhip zipped him, too. Pop broke in his new shillelagh. *Shi-lay-lee.* Forged by an Irish witch! Trumpets exploded! I bolted to the front window. Galloglasses gathered in the street. Howled in unison the Walsh clan war cry, "Pierced through, but not dead!"

I rattled! Phoned Jesus. He was bombing a screen test and sent St. Thomas in his stead, but he got creamed by a milk truck. Sunday afternoon plumes. Exodus Eve. Mom and the kids were out. Pop was there, a mushroom cloud! He sprayed rat poison. Defamations. Cornered me in the kitchen.

"You're never going to—"

I ran to him shaking, shrieked, "Can't you see? I'm scared as hell!" I began to cry.

Pop drooped. Wrapped me in a bear hug. Wept. John G. never cried! His head guillotined, leprechauns and handmaidens poured from his neck. Tossing clover! Corned beef! I was shocked. Euphoric. A revelation! He was terrified I'd get mauled out West.

Remembered that it hadn't always been snuff-film matinees with me and Pop playing leads. He was blunt as a judge, honest as a day's work, incorruptible as a bodhisattva. He held us kids to high—at times impossible—standards. But he blew trumpets! Ushered me into starry worlds of poker, ice cream parlors, baseball, cinema. Took me to my first film when I was five, *The Sound Of Music*. I was a Roman candle! The grand theater. Its immense screen. Buttered popcorn. Candy bars big as gold bricks! Pop's strong hand gentle on my shoulder guided me to my seat.

8

January, thirty below zero. My adieu! Manic! Moony! Raw as bloody pork chops. Primed for sodomy. Bacteria! A fleecing! Oblivion awaited! Othello! Tore up my season tickets to Pop's funhouse. Stuffed Scout's postcard into my billfold along with his yearbook pic.

Mom and Pop in the driveway. Stoic. Eternal. We hugged.

"I'm your man," Pop whispered in my ear.

Whipped Caballo, who peed antifreeze and limped southwest. Pop's cherubim squatted on one shoulder. D's talons mangled the other. I was going to pummel D, lacerate it, stand over it triumphant. If death awaited me? Why not?

"Set crosses along the roadside to San Diego for Michael," Mother petitioned the Lord.

I used them for firewood. As daggers. South of Des Moines, a sign on Johnny Appleseed Highway blinked "Burn a flag: $25 Fine. Burn a Vietnamese: $25 Bounty. Sponsored by Iowa Citizens for Moderation." Oh, noble Heartland! Lady Liberty's clogged viscera! A line of Somali refugees tramped the shoulder. Marbled. Bloodshot. Factory-ready.

Paint threw a shoe in the Indianola dusk. Wap! Wap! Pulled into Standard Oil. Winchester pickups. Blood-bank pies. Busted Coke machine—filled with sucker fish. Expired aspirations. Next door, the Greyhound station blipped want-to-go-west dreamers. Dorothy. Li'l Abner. Son of Sam. Shadows squealed with runaways giving line drivers blow jobs.

I pounded Schlitz at the counter of the Glow-Bug Diner across the street while the blacksmiths jacked Caballo. Plastic pioneers puffed in and out. Loquacious losers. Porno saints. AWOL soldiers frizzing the corsage smiles of the waitresses. A sea turtle woman scraped past me. She licked the wallpaper. Clomped up buckwheat stairs to a second floor tenement. Clawing sand with her rosary knuckles. Blue numbers chicken flesh. Opened her door. Room tight as her social security check. Her old beau waiting to die. Tube rays gushed a morphine river.

On Standard's other side, juke joint blew. Jesus at half mast. Black men shivered in doorway. Crying out electric! Across the street, the Acme Hero Factory spit out three shifts.

A bony mechanic elbowed me. Jibbered, "Last week. Ray Fine. Manager over yonder at Acme. Shot his wife, three kids. Then he drove to the Pella VFW rib feed. Polished off two racks. Then, while he was nobbing some gook whore, had a goddamn heart attack and died." He smiled wickedly. Moseyed to the john. Vaporized.

I cracked another Schlitz. Glow-Bug pot roast. Mashed potatoes. Slept in the bus station.

Cold cuts and root beer in Dodge City. Met some local buckaroos who flaunted Leavenworth tattoos. Hot rods. They sized me up. Stripped off my shirt. Cackled over Pop's red rubber stamp on my ribs: "U.S. Canner grade." Two-day pillow at con's flop. Torched the Chinese pipe. Black gas! Black Velvet. *White Light/White Heat.*

Scrammed at werewolf. Prairie billboards blazed. South of Wild Bill, yellow dogs crabbed to holding pens beneath a fiery beacon that read "Is Jesus Here?" Quarter mile, another read "Touchy Feely!" in gigantic white script over a red background. And in smaller print: "Billy the Kid's Penis—350 miles—Las Vegas, New Mexico." I roared!

Los Alamos, a charred blue daybreak. Discount gas masks. Zap fences. Nuke-test chimps screamed from inside cages along the roadside. They tossed shit and nailed Caballo's hood. I spun into Atomic Al's Nuclear Supply, housed in an abandoned Piggly Wiggly. A sign over the compound read "Dear Japan, We're Sorry for the Atomic Bomb." I fizzed. Lucid. Woolly. Ready for specimens. I poked through the littered debris field that surrounded Atomic Al's. Plastic skeletons. Truman's parachute. Russian nuke equipment. Spools of piano wire. Martian flags.

Atomic Al gushed out of a vacuum chamber. He was gussied up in a cardinal's red cassock. Silver cross around his neck big enough to brain a Mormon. He gleamed, took off his bloody biretta, bowed, and said, "Just in time, lab rat. Join me in celebrating at my First Church of Manhattan."

"I'm radioactive."

"Fuel rod glows, does it?" he chuckled, made the sign of the cross, motioned me to follow, turned, and disappeared past x-ray converter bomb casings.

I ran after him. Flashed Othello's picture.

Atomic cocked his head, squinted, and snarled, "Who be you?"

"Mike." I scrounged Othello's postcard from my wallet as well. Forked it.

"Uh-huh," he muttered, looking me over. "Elroy Jetson. Kid could use a friend."

"Is he here?"

"He worked here a month. Slept in one of my bomb shelters. Vanished six months ago."

"Why?"

"Don't know." He looked off in thought. "Well—"

"What?"

He leaned against an electric chair. "A while back I sent the president two cans of Organic Plutonium."

I laughed.

"FBI showed," he cracked. "Bastards beetled all over! Elroy was gone the next day."

"Any idea where?"

"Come on inside," he said, ignoring my Q, turned, and headed into the gutted-out Piggly Wiggly.

I loafed in the aisles. Lazarus gauges. Oh Boy! goggles. Annihilation badges. Spy cameras. Thermocouples. Skin graft kits. Oscilloscopes. Invisible cemetery plots.

Atomic fingered a Geiger counter and barked, "Drop your pants." Ran the meter from my knees to my tonsils. It blabbed silly. I teetered.

"Congratulations, lab rat! You're a radioactive son of a gun."

"You've got it rigged!" I hollered.

Atomic smiled devilishly. Laughed. "My congregation awaits me," he yawped. He strode past a fluorescent cow, turned, and said with a wink, "Stick around. I'll be back."

"Okay," I said half excited. I ambled out to Caballo.

Jerked off in a quart of Oly. Thirty minutes wilted. Atomic rapped paint's blinder. Hopalong Cassidy! Missouri shirt. Rattlesnake bolo tie. Chaps.

He splashed a two-dollar smile and said morosely, "A local college gal from Albuquerque turned up murdered not long after Elroy arrived. Sheriffs found the body in the desert two, three miles from here. Stabbed a dozen times."

"Oh?"

"After Elroy left, I found her school ID in his bomb shelter. Never showed it to the cops." Atomic scratched his head, raked me, looked me dead red and drawled, "Elroy didn't seem cut out for killing."

"Uh-huh," I replied softly. Bloody Shriner/Howard gave me a sloppy smooch! I saw Othello brandishing his knife. Big as a machete! Carving up a coed! My guts plopped out onto the Manson Family scrapbook. Flashed Scout whacking Shriner—three times! The terrible sound of the head splitting! Did I love Othello too much that I couldn't see the truth? Hell, he even said he'd thought about killing Howard in the bar. No!

"What you going to do with the ID?" I asked weakly.

"Haven't decided. Hell, I liked the kid. I've been hoping they catch the killer so I can burn the damn thing." He crossed his arms across his wind bag, looked off, and said, "Don't feel too good about the notion of handing the ID to the sheriff with a story of some phantom kid who slept in my bomb shelter. They'd love nothing more than to implicate me and shut this place down. You can imagine I'm not very popular with the Catholic Church or the feds at the death factory."

He turned, ambled away, and disappeared into Piggly Wiggly. Followed him inside. Bet he wrote down my license plate number! Bought a Geiger counter. Gas mask. Two cans of Organic Plutonium. Ate one in the parking lot. Tasted a lot like cream of mushroom soup. Revved Caballo.

Atomic trotted to my window. "Take this, will you?" he said with pleading eyes. Slid me the dead girl's ID.

"Awful hot, ain't it?"

"Hot as Venus," he drawled.

I scoured the old man's face for lies. Didn't find any. Atomic exhaled. He smiled and walked away. I studied the ID. Maria Sanchez. Pretty girl. Shoved it under the floorboards.

Set spurs to my nag. I had to find Othello. Atomic said the girl was killed not long after Scout's arrival. Was he hunkered somewhere in Los Alamos? Scenes flashed of our blood pact at Radio Dada. Scout's sobbing face. His fear. He relied on me. On me! Undaunted, I spent the next three days in Los Alamos. Combed bars. Whorehouses. Pool rooms. Slept in Caballo. The dead girl's ID under my floorboards smoked, licked my feet with flames. No sign of Othello. I didn't dare flash his picture, fearing I'd get arrested in connection with the coed's murder. Guessed he'd probably blown Los Alamos. If he hadn't aced Maria, he may have gotten wind of the crime or seen it on the news and figured he'd be a prime suspect.

I blew town. Happy as clotted blood. I hoped Othello would fire another postcard Mom and Pop's way. Until then, nothing I could do.

9

The Geiger counter on the front seat chirped Russian the whole goddamned way to Highway 85 South. Another of Atomic Al's jokes? I stopped in Truth or Consequences. Twila at the Drift Motel. Fifteen-year-old Reno runaway. Suitcase filled with alligator teeth. Forged checks. Legs like birthday candles. She threw on the gas mask. I couldn't get it up. She clawed my cheek in wet-pussy throes.

Next morn, I found an abandoned Malibu Barbie doll in a rest-stop toilet outside Las Cruces. Her bikini torn off. A cig butt jammed up her ass. I fixed her up. Promised her wine and roses. We were married on the spot. I propped her on the dash. Horseshoes and tequila in the shade in Wilcox, Arizona. South at Dead Mule. Took Ice Road past a radio tower to McNeal. Geronimo Trailer Park. Eucalyptus. Bleached dreams. Poker game picnic table behind Phillips 66. Monster movies flickering across the back wall. My new companions were plaid men. Staid. Repentant. Winchesters in their laps. Dealt cards with indigo fingernails. Uneasy laughter. Nearby, inside the trailer, their vodka wives leaned into rubber turns in zoo skates and Wichita helmets.

Caballo snapped a tendon west of Pirtleville. I pissed on his head. Coasted to a deserted Mobil station. Shoved Barbie into my britches, grabbed my duffel, the dead girl's ID, and torched the nag. Black smoke womp-womp. Hooves flayed Kentucky. Walked across the border to Agua Prieta. Found the Carnival Room. Mescal. Pranced Liberace loafers. Buzzcocked a local cocheta. She wore a gun belt. Bucked badgers. Her Absolut perfume conjured Flo Bolen. Guilt's coals! Scenes of Flo smooching Othello's postcard!—Flo in hot fishnets! Closed my eyes and slobbered her French furs while Cocheta zapped my transistor.

The sun bled. I walked armadillo. Service road crackled. Caballo billowed as I slid past the Mobil a furlong to Dot's Cafe. Cocheta echoed. I tugged at my prick. Ordered Dot's Special: Huevos rancheros. Borax shake.

A Mexican shiny-Sunday-chapel family sat in the booth across the aisle. Three girls between five and dime. The youngest leaned over, eyed Malibu sunning next to my bubbling shake.

"Boys can't have Barbies," she sassed and started to giggle. Her folks hee-heed. Twitched. Waited for my knee jerk.

"She's my wife," I said. Everyone chuckled.

"We're on vacation!" proclaimed the girl.

"Where you—?"

"Disneyland!" yipped all three sisters.

"I'm going to kiss Mickey Mouse," said sister number two.

"You smell!" giggled the youngest.

"Joaquina!" snapped her mother. Her father smiled apologetically.

"Must have been that cougar I wrestled back in McNeal."

"Really?" oohed Joaquina.

"He was a big one, all right."

"Where you going?" asked sister number one.

"San Diego."

"Don't go to 'The Thing!'" sister number two whispered loudly.

"It's a raunchy tourist trap!" Joaquina shouted. "Just an old mummy in a glass case."

Everyone laughed.

I followed the saints out ten minutes later. They buzzed around a yellow Ford wagon. I waved. Headed across the parking lot for 80 Bisbee.

The girls pulled Papa's pant leg, pointed at me, and begged, "Can't he? Come on, Papa! Can't he?"

Papa rolled. Beelined toward me. Just then a coyote zigged out of the brush. It ran up to Mama and the girls and stopped. They all spooked. Mama SOSed Jesus. The mutt turned, looked at me, and cocked its head to one side. A distinct black patch covered one eye. It spun toward the family and darted back into the sage. Papa one-eightied, ran back and shoved the girls into the wagon. They sped off.

I shrugged. Never moped when a ride jilted me. The road was more than my best girl. More than a salve for my depression. I was her pupil. An apprentice of erotica! Benevolence! American neuroses! I was a glutton for experience. Collector of philosophies. Specimens—Barbie dolls—ephemera—one-nighters. I was a specimen. That's where my treasure lay. The intoxication of hurling myself forward, out there. The wonder of a total stranger pulling over. The anticipation before the door popped open and I met my prize. The bon voyage!

Lit a cheroot. Mohawked a quarter mile to an abandoned adobe. Sat on my duffel in the shade. An hour ticked. A '64 silver-black Cadillac hearse made dust. An electric window hummed. I walked up. An Apache split with a pitted sandstone face and a beaverskin hat. Rough-rider blouse. Fifty winters. On the dash, a brown scorpion in a glass container, wire mesh top. The Apache dragged her turquoise claws over her coffin-in-tow. Ran her orbs over my branches.

"An owl told me about you," she said, matter-of-fact. "The sad wandering redbeard who burned his car." She flicked the passenger door open.

I peered inside. Studied the killer. "How far?"

She looked off into the sage. "The Spanish called the Sonora

'Camino del Diablo.'"

No entiendo showed in my mug.

"The Devil's Highway. This stretch used to be the Butterfield stage coach route," she huffed. "Lots of killing."

"Uh-huh."

"Where you headed, honcho?"

"Ocean."

"I'm picking up a stiff for a burial in El Centro."

Plasma pumped! El Centro twinkled along the Arizona-California border! I tossed my duffel on the floorboard and climbed in. Stared at the scorpion.

"My sister," she said.

"Boyfriend?"

"Ate the last one. Head first."

"I meant you."

"Ate the last one. Head first," she tittered.

I smiled, went mute. I liked this one! A witch?

"She's a bark scorpion. The most lethal in North America. Poison is a neurotoxin, like the venom from a cobra or coral snake. Kill a thousand people in Mexico each year."

"How many she killed?"

Apache smiled a pixie smile. Reached between my knees and popped the glove box.

"Always carry two vials of antivenin."

I eyed the bottles and hypo.

"Scorpions are also quite resilient. After nuke tests in White Sands, scientists found them near ground zero with no adverse effects."

"Dandy."

We rode dumb for half a cheroot.

"The owl also said that you'd probably die today," she finally said. "But you should be happy, because your life has been like a lost fawn scampering through a brush fire."

My kisser carbonized. But only for a second. Her tough talk was beginning to bore me.

We blazed Devil's Highway toward Bisbee. Tombstone. Dozed in, out. Cactus. Barbed wire. Bullet-riddled cars. Folks

I'd hurt camped along the roadside in cardboard hovels. Dutch ovens fuming. I waved bony traitor knuckles.

Apache scratched my shoulder. Purred, "Sleep in the coffin, if you like."

"Really?" I yawned.

She pulled over. I shuffled. Creaked the double doors. Crawled into the whale vagina. Plush! Forget-me-nots. Howard's corpse in a Twinkie suit. Fez. Eyes open. Head-jelly leaked.

"Go ahead," the Apache said. "I know you want to."

"What?"

"Close the lid."

I did.

Una hora. Una tenido pesadilla. One hour. One bad dream. Father Glinka's pearly Buick in Pop's driveway. The Russian priest only made house calls for last rites or castrations! Glinka lurked in milkweed! In my Trojans! Pop—my Irish Lord—was perched on his blackthorn cathedra—behind stone walls and moss—pounding my sins into Father Glinka's forehead with a shillelagh. *Shi-lay-lee.* Hounds brayed. I was a crow with a belly full of Land O' Lakes sweet corn, too fat to fly.

Glinka said, "We're trying to guide Michael gently, but that's not why I came—"

"Gently! 'Ten Hail Marys' is for fairies and sophists!" cried the old man, spewing badger snot on the padre's booze blossoms. "Dish out penance to the lad like Spanish lightning! You and your Jesuits over at the rectory with your color TVs and La-Z-Boys getting fat off my bread while I bust my ass! I've sweated a Sea of Galilee since '51! Lean on that boy with the brawn of Samson, follow?"

Father Glinka smiled impishly. "I came here to tell you that I've heard rumors of Michael being involved in some awful business in St. Paul. You see, a man was murdered and—"

"Rumors tumors! This burg invented gossip! If I had a dollar for every rumor I've heard about that boy I could buy a cake-eater mansion in Edina. Telling me this out of the kindness of your heart? Or because I tithe enough to put angels in cashmere sweaters and Prada loafers?"

"Doctor Walsh, really? No, no, no."

"Michael?" Pop thundered, spun around.

I tore feathers behind a pile of toe tags. Whizzed on Pop's Glenn Miller records. Brownies scurried in codpieces and corsages—carrying bundles of femurs to the powder house. Marrow machines wheezed. Groaned. Carnival dogs dragged entrails. Police call boxes blazed along County Road 3! Along the periphery, Flashlight City rangers bitched about their wives into walkie-talkies. Bloodhounds spidered out of Pop's robes! But somehow the old man couldn't see me!

"I'll interview the boy!" Pop bellowed, gave the pastor's skull a playful ding, leaned back and rumbled, "If he had anything to do with a murder, I'll strip the bark off that boy and send him to your holy mill, Father, ready for finishing."

I woke, popped lid. Weaseled around. Saw a sign for Gila Bend. Underneath: "Yuma 50 Miles." Lay back down just before the brakes cried. Coffin smacked against the front seat. Sirens flashed their red tickers through the windshield. I sat up. Cops' radio blab outside. Blood-spattered sun. The Apache wove through the rubberneckers until we passed a yellow Ford wagon. Ripped in two! Mama caught in the shark jaws of the jagged windshield. Papa and sisters one through three strewn across the highway, covered now with sheets. I fossilized.

The Apache veered onto the shoulder and skidded to a stop. The black-eye coyote from Dot's Special appeared next to the right fender! Apache flung the passenger door open. It hopped inside. The Apache grabbed the scorpion cage and took its top off. The coyote stuck its snout into the cage and quickly jumped into the back. I pressed back into the coffin with fright. Coyote hovered over me. I smelled musk. Death. Fell into its black eyes. Its snout tickled mine. It unrolled its ivory tongue.

The scorpion dropped onto my heart-box. The Apache cackled. The coffin lid Caesared. Couldn't open it! It sank into Pearl Harbor, but fire stung my shoulder. I screamed. Crushed the scorpion against my collar bone. But not before the rubber mallet to the funny bone on my left side. The shades came down. I fell into warm oil. Dreamed blue men chained to metal desks.

Hundreds! Fingernails scratching mute petitions.

Awoke in pig's entrails, the slippery inside of the coffin. I needed to piss! There was an SOS pad stuffed down my gullet. But I could feel my arms! Marvelous legs! I was naked. I hammered on the inside of the coffin lid. Heave-hoed. It was heavy! I was weak. Limp as a prick. Only Fiona's Flea Circus could've busted out. I blabbed to the angels. To Pop! My lungs echoed. How much sand had run through the hour glass? Days! Spermatozoa half-lives! There were no wheels underneath me tugging pavement. Where was I? The Apache? I listened for the sound of her nails. Nothing.

I waited. Blubbered, "I'm a volcano! I'm a maggot!" No prizes. Tongue on chin. An hour slid. When the Reaper's knuckles tapped a dirge on my throat, I blew a whistle! Awoke the gypsy boys dozing in my gut furnace. The lot slippery as Vaseline. A band of rejects! Cock pullers! Innocent cuties mugging in banshee masks! Bashing flutophones. Ripping out each other's hair. We mumbled spontaneous prayers. Litanies of lust.

"Holy! Holy! Moly!" we sang in unison. "Holy fucking moly! All at once, now, goddamn it! That's it!"

We skunked Hercules's balls. Lid flew open! The weight on top of us smacked onto the floor. Blowfish mouth sucking wind! Blind as a believer, I belly-flopped over the side! Flailing legs. Snot. Horse hair. Thwack into a pile of wet seedpods and muddy roots. Sat up. A sweet fragrance! Dim light through a stained-glass window! My eyes adjusted. A small room. A crypt! The coffin perched on sawhorses. I looked through horse legs. Hundreds of yellow lotus flowers piled on the floor! That's what had been on top of me!

Felt skinny as bacon. Tried to stand. Legs flaccid. Rose finally, slimy as newborn moose dope. Lunged over to drool on the stained glass. A window-door! Lowered my shoulder. Door blew. Chains clanged. Dawn peeled. My cemetery! My resurrection! I lifted my arms. Danced! Sang! Yipped! Pissed Preakness against a headstone. Spooked in case of grave diggers. Derelicts. None! Only the sweet dead! Dashed to a garden hose. Filled camel hump. Scurried back inside. Stuck my head back in the coffin. My wallet! DL! Traveler's checks! All there! Crunch! The empty antivenin vial and the needle. Apache!

Sun flamed. I panicked! Needed duds before Alice Cooper's roadies bloomed. They'd fuck me in the ass! Roll me in lime! Make me a stage prop. Or worse! The cops would splash in, shitting psych-ward tickets. Crew-cut floor monitors! Restraints! Hypodermics! Colonic starter kits! Hysterical phone calls to Pop! *You call crying, and I'll think about sending a bus ticket to whatever damn town you chicken out in.*

Who would believe my tale? Scanned my cell. There were four apartments in the crypt. One was open. It was empty! Blank nameplate. Intended for me? Nameplate on the apartment to its right read "Charles 'Busby' Lions. Loving Husband and Father. Born 1888. Died 1926." I donned pot holders. Opened musty Pillsbury oven. Pulled out Chuck's muffins. The stench sucker-punched me! A tassel of gray hair clung to a blackened skull like weeds sprouting after a firestorm. Blue pinstripe suit. Forty-two long. Stacy Adams! Banker's trou. Fondling cold meat is tricky business, but Chuck was quickly fleeced. Bones snapped. Dust flew. Fast as a cheating wolf, I jumped into Stacy's. Stuffed my wallet into the inside jacket pocket. Tucked Charles into bed again. Peeped outside. No shovel boys! Crammed lotuses into my pockets. One behind each ear. I sped outside.

Froze at the placard on the crypt's door: "10 a.m. burial. Monday, January 30. Deceased: John Doe. Vault donated by family. Evergreen Cemetery—El Centro, California."

Remembered the Sunday family in the yellow Ford wagon. Today was Monday! Heard Apache's voice, "Picking up a stiff for a burial in El Centro." It was me! I was the stiff! If I hadn't woken up, I would've been a goner! Sealed inside the apartment by the cemetery crew! Why? Was the Apache witch offering only death or also transfiguration? Ecstasy? A newborn appreciation for life? Lotus flowers, a symbol of death or of rebirth? The coyote, another witch? How had it hoofed from Dot's Special to the accident scene so quickly? If the black-eye hadn't spooked the Mexican family, I might have wound up under a sheet on the highway.

Maybe it was simpler—the Apache was a sadist, a psychopathic killer.

I didn't care! Didn't regret it! I grabbed stars! Danced! Giddy, skipped through the gravestones like a fairy field kid. Found cemetery road. Long as a Tiparillo. Smoked it down. Bolted through the front gate.

10

Walked west to East Orange. Mottled. Daffy. Dignified as dirt.
An alien in dead man's clothes. I had no language. Grunts.
Spittle. Green shit. Groves of TV antennas buzzed. I floated
north along East Main. A finger bone fell out of my pocket.
Popped into a blinky AM PM Market. Hyena sandwich. Quart
shellac. I sparked an Old Gold and high-stepped down East
Main. Drones hive-humped. Toyotas stuffed with fish guts and
unpaid bills. Sun winced. My suit was speckled with embalming fluid. Custard. Brain-matter. Peeled for Johnny Boy
Scouts. I jumped to West Commercial. Bums. Nuns. Factory
whistles. Varicose shift hemorrhaged into parking lots. Working joes with psoriasis. Sickle cell. Coin-operated pensions.
The American dream!—trapped! Suffocating like moths in
mayonnaise jars! Up ahead a train flickered between crackerbox houses! I wanted to get the hell out of El Centro! I ran
hee-hee straitjacket to the deadhead. Union Pacific yard! Bouquets of coal! Grease! Desperadoes! I dodged a brakemen in
Wild Turkey coveralls. Boxcars batted their eyes! I rubbed skin

along a sleeping rattler. Open car! Flapped new-kid wings. Stuck my head inside.

"Beat it road kid," growled a fat harelip, "or cough up a fin!"

I whistled happily. Tossed Fatty a lotus.

There was a songbird in the next car. A sable wanderer. One eye. One arm. Lounged on a Washington Apple throne. He smiled. Scratched his gray beard.

"Hey, Bo. Never mind Idaho Bob." He oozed molasses. "His angelina, uh, his road kid nailed a Bloody Nose to Texas last week. Been a son of a bitch since."

"Uh-huh," I shrugged, indifferent. "San Diego?"

He waved me in. Soaped, "Yes, prushin, this freight's a big hole in the sky."

I fluttered inside. Dropped onto a crate opposite the saint.

He eyeballed my lion suit. Embalming fluid socked him in the nose. "Holy Jesus! Your glad rags need boiling up."

"And how."

"We'll pick up cadavers in Plaster City." He drained his bottle of shine. Tossed it to the floorboards. "Fifteen pancakes. Gila-monster route croaks there. SD&A will get you to Fairy Town." He looked forlornly at the dead soldier. "Good town to beach tramp. Clowns or bulls spot you?"

"Who?"

"Brakemen, company dicks."

"No."

"First time punching the breeze?"

I nodded. His beard split, his smile parading yellow piano keys.

"First time I rode the blinds, my dick could've darned socks," he laughed. "I'm Blue Note Davis. You?"

"Muckle."

He caught me eyeing his stump.

"Played the sax!" he cawed. "I wasn't Charlie Parker, but boy, I could climb clouds!" He donned soot. Whispered, "Hit and run in Detroit. Was only twenty-two."

"I'm sorry."

"You should nomad with me."

"Where?"

His face lit up again. "We can jungle in the Big Rock Candy Mountains!"

I smiled.

"Any hooch?"

"Had some scorpion antivenin, but I shot it all."

He chuckled and then settled back and cut to dreamland. The hurricane shuddered! Clanked! Rolled out! City hubbub. I sat in the open doorway. Jubilant! Resurrected! Lusty as a bull! A warm breeze. An azure sky. The city faded. We crawled across a Thomas Cole canvas. Rose fields to the horizon! Five miles click-clack. Bloated lettuce fields puked Mexican braceros—swinging *los cortitos*, short-handled hoes. At Arm & Hammer I'd read about the braceros' harsh life. Imagined Cheez Whiz bosses. Shiny pickups. Rolexes. Stetsons. Watching through Winchester .30-30 scopes. Sheep-head stew lunch in truck bed. In the heat-rippled distance, workers' families played hangman in squatter huts. Alfalfa covered Seeley, Dixieland like fur coats on Okies. I smoked two cigs, and we reached Plaster City, a botched nuke test of a town. Zombies did the rumba in Gypsum Hills.

We screeched into the yard. Blue Note hustled me into an empty boxcar on a beachcomber special.

"Wait till you see Goat Canyon Trestle!" he cried over his shoulder as he skidded down the line.

"Okay! Thanks!"

Crawled through tunnels, up switchbacks. An hour breezed. Carrizo Gorge. A barren old cunt. Trestles pinched mountain peaks like garters on amputated legs. Vistas! Salutations! Erections! Creaked across the Goat Canyon Trestle. Two-hundred-foot drop! Imagined cutthroats' corpses hemp swinging. Crossed the border at Division, on to Tecate, Mantanuco, TJ. Then San Diego! I bailed in the National City yard. My Xanadu! My new bosom! Loped to the Highway 5 on-ramp. Kissed tar.

A '53 Mercury woodie scratched the shoulder. An alabaster mailman at the wheel. "Swagman!" he yelled, hit a J. "Ocean Beach! Hey! Can take you!"

I hopped in. He passed the reefer.

"I'm Dean," he said. "Acid run. Just came from Imperial Beach. Two hundreds hits. King you?"

"Uh, thanks. Not right now." Hoped I could mooch a sofa. "Live in Ocean Beach?"

"Nah. My girlfriend. She's a married gal. Husband's a marriage counselor."

"Hah!"

"Where'd you get the funky suit?"

"Off a dead man."

He laughed.

Dusk. Dean tossed me onto Newport Avenue.

"Here." He handed me two hits. "OB!" he laughed. "Gnarly!" He blew away.

The sea! Heaved! Boiled! Serenaded! Sashayed toward Poseidon! Jibbering praises, dirty ditties! VW bus—a woolly mammoth—approached behind me, trumpeted! I spun. Its crankcase fizzing Protestants. Captain wore x-ray specs. Mama Cass choker. Held a J the size of Nixon's war dick.

"Come on!" he waved. "Room for one more!"

The VW door slid open. Sammy surfer. Hell's Angels duo. Coked-up MD. Three Frisbee dogs. A Hare Krishna. A topless, leathery sunflower beach queen. A sweaty seraphim tweaker slapping bluebird wallpaper onto the ceiling. I got in. X-ray zoomed. Newport deadheaded into Abbott. He swung a roscoe.

"There she blows!" he yipped, braked. "Look! Just north of the pier!"

We leeched the windows. I didn't see anything.

"Our prize!" shouted the beach queen. "Look near the jetty, past the surfers. Five beached executives. Nailed naked. Swept into the dazzling La Jolla sea foam. Floating past belly-up. Tasting the cold hammer."

"That's twenty-six this month!" squealed X-ray.

I still didn't see anything.

"Foggy's Notion, ho!" shouted one of the Angels. "First round on me!"

Everyone flung orchids.

Zeed on the beach for three moons. Sex Wax cot in Billy's Surfboard Shop. Took a factory job. Hara-kiri Engineer. Psychosis Department. Boss Bob Bone. Wino. Twit. Connoisseur of excretions and bestiality films. I saved up to rent a Pacific Beach flop-room off Garnet. Flaming oriental. Cockroaches. Section Eight wombs. Bought some secondhand clothes. Had my El Centro cemetery suit Martinized. Crammed it into my souvenir closet. Murdered Bob Bone in dreams. Quit after six months. Rented a room in a Morena shack with two other young cats. I strangled shovel jobs out of Laborers Local No. 89. The ducats were prime, but work was streaky. My Xanadu was a wreck. Man's cruelty buzz-sawed here just like any place else. Pop had warned me: "A murderous harbor!—lush!—desolate!—a diseased wonderland!" I was a fool.

D's claws tore my tripe to Tangiers. Booze, pot, women, game-show hosts shot out. Stuffed them back inside. The same cycle here as anywhere. Scenes spun behind my eyes. Prickly AZ. Jacked off to the Apache. The bloody Mexican family ogled.

11

January '81. Reagan inaugurated. China dilated. Hoodwinks! Wall Street crooks handed the keys to Treasury Department. Deregulation! Blow jobs all around. Toasts of bull semen! Hooray! Smarmy violins. Smirks. Factories died. My paychecks? Guillotined! My union laborer's shovel? Quarantined! Egg sandwiches. Pinto beans.

June fizzed. My fellow tomcats scrammed. I couldn't pay the rent. Insomnia. Bathtub gin. Alka Seltzer. Two week loop. Ready to ditch. A surfer rolled into the shack on an eight-ball of blow. Wallet stuffed with rhino.

"Heard you were scrambling for new skeletons," he drawled and cracked a beatific smile that would've made Kerouac genuflect.

"That's right."

He flipped up his aviators, patted his Hawaiian shirt. "I'm Lance. I can cover the rent for the next two months. No hassy."

I raised the ceiling with an eyebrow. "What's the catch?"

He smiled. "No hassy."

Sent Jack to his knee again. He moved in five minutes later.

Lance Ryan was thirty. Ten tree rings up. Eyes of a cherub. Soul of a Comanche medicine man. At seventeen Lance cut the face off a dead Iroquois. The tail off a panther. Slapped them on. Rambled the beach for doxy and disciples. He bagged plenty—became alpha male of a group of flower children. He'd been a VW mechanic the past ten years. Tinkered with Baja Bugs and girls at his dumpy shop in Pacific Beach. His prize was Suzie. His sadistic empress. A half-Russian Nigerian. Days of straps and hoses! Days of bloody noses! Days of cries and roses! And he loved her forevermore! Suzie screamed obscenities and catcalls! Sent him moaning over the falls! Smeared his dreams all over the walls! And he loved her forevermore! When the moon bulged, they'd bolt Lance's bedroom door. Blow horns! Recite lines from *Who's Afraid of Virginia Wolf*. Suzie, in black latex, strutted, waving a horse whip. She hung him upside down. Lashes! Rumbles! Shrieks! The floor shook!

"Oh, heaven," he warbled. "I'm in heaven!"

How do I know? He goaded me into hiding in his closet. One session made me puke.

Lance and I slopped in beach breakfast joints. Deep-sea fishing. Barbecues with his comrades. I shoved him onto a crate because of his code: Fuck the government. Have no bank accounts or social security number. Live life by your own rules.

"Go by your feelings," he told me.

April Fools? I woke at three to piss. Spied into Lance's bedroom as I passed by. On his bed, kilos of cocaine. Stacked like Khufu's pyramid. Pile of twenty-dollar bills. The muffled voice of a stranger. In the crapper I was so shook up I could barely shake off. I heard Jesus bellowing curses. Sirens. Whirlybirds. A plea droned through a bullhorn! I'd get the slammer. Mom and Pop at my trial. Sweating rosaries. Donned in shame. Disappointment. I had visions of prison. Diseased cellmates named Screw and Hippo. I listened. Mumbles. A laugh. I waited for death. The click of a .38's hammer. Then silence. I slipped back to my room unnoticed.

A month blew. Insomnia returned. Swinging an ax. A blowtorch. I'd shed pounds. Sympathy. Bang! Poof! Dead angels came screaming through the roof. Lance flung them into the furnace. Snorted their ashes. Syringes and blood spatter in Lance's john. He'd started banging. Cocaine shrunk him. Marooned him. He hired the Sex Pistols' make-up artist. His flower children scattered. He'd only worm out of his bedroom to eat or shoot up, hurling knives at me. They didn't miss. Now I was Loser, Asshole, Fucking Tourist. Blamed me for world famine, cancer, fucking tracks on his arms. Treated me like his houseboy. I grew to hate my Mr. Hyde. My fallen hero. I felt skinned alive. Trampled. I was naive, unable to understand the Devil of addiction.

I beat it. It was the end of August. I butterflied girls' couches at the beach. Lance died two weeks later. Crushed by a speedball, a lightning bolt of cocaine and heroin. Cops found him naked in bed, bowl of Lucky Charms on the nightstand, his white German Shepherd sitting vigilant. I went to the Point Loma burial. Hippie mourners heaved rip tide. I didn't then. Was still fuming. Only reason I attended was to see friends I'd met through Lance.

My walkie-talkie echoed a week later.

"You got a postcard, friend."

"Pop." Othello! "What's it say?"

"M-u-r-d-e-r."

I fell out of the sky. Splat in the middle of a Shriner's parade. Pop stood over me, breathing through a muzzle.

"The card's blank. It's from your chum, Bolen, isn't it?"

"I can't—"

"St. Paul gumshoes came by for crumpets and cake. They droned on about a masquerader from the Guthrie with an eternal headache. Got their money on Bolen. Were you there? Don't tell me. I lied so much about the postcard and your whereabouts that I've had to pay rent at the confessional."

"I'm sorry to get you guys—"

"Your mother lit a wall of candles for you at the parish. The goddamn place burned down." A bullwhip cracked.

"The postmark?"

"King City, California. August third." He took a slug of something. I guessed Irish Mist. "Last time you saw the fugitive?"

"Before he blew Land O' Lakes."

"Going to King City, aren't you?"

"Yeah."

"Odds you make it back unscathed?"

"Five to one."

"Jesus and Joseph! Twenty to one, unless your track record and your judgment have miraculously improved. Have they, friend?"

I sucked mothballs.

"Life ain't a bowl of cherries."

"Uh-huh."

"When you going to give us a visit?" His voice gone small.

"Don't know."

Silence.

"Talk to your mother," he whispered.

"Mike, it's Mom. Wait. Okay, he's out of the room now. Your father's gone completely out of his mind. He's been so worried about you that he called the Vatican and tried to arrange a blessing from the Pope. A novena or something! He promised to do charity work for cripples in Bangladesh. Give up all his possessions. Even the Electra 225. My God, he's sleeptalking in Gaelic. He hasn't done that since NBC cancelled *Sing Along with Mitch*. I don't know what I'm going to do. He made me cook Johnny Marzetti four times this week. Wait, I think he's—no it's okay."

"He's convinced I was involved in the murder, isn't he?"

"He's rolled it around a couple million times."

"And you?"

"No."

I sighed with relief. "What did the police say?"

"They were pretty tight-lipped. Asked how much time you spent with Othello and things like that. They made the rounds. Questioned a half dozen of Othello's other friends and their parents."

"Tell Pop I'm enlisting in the French Foreign Legion."

She laughed. "Oh, he's back. Okay, uh, your father wants to say something. Love you."

"Love you, too."

Pop thundered, "There's an Irish saying, *On tay a lee-on le maw-dee aye-rogue shay le darnid. He who lies down with dogs gets up with fleas.* Good luck, Muckle, on your journey to King City." Talking with Pop was always Dublin in the rain. We only spoke on birthdays and execution days. I still hadn't wised up about how life had coldcocked him. Howard's killing gave him a sunburn. I tried to shake off the guilt. Not a chance. Hit Old Crow. Sparked a Bubonic. I ached for phosphorous. Pork. Nietzsche's Zarathustra! His greasy overman! His swollen erectus! To excavate my soul, gas it up with Gothic fight songs. Wolves! Stuff me into a Long Tom! Aim toward Beatitude's crystal fields! Kaboom!

I eyed a map. King City, sixty miles south of Monterey. I'd never told Mrs. Bolen shit. But I flushed my promise to Othello and tapped the walkie-talkie.

"Mrs. Bolen. It's Mike."

Ice tinkled in a glass. "Fuck! Mike!" she slurred. "It's not Christmas! What the h—!"

"Othello's alive."

The phone dropped. She gurgled dog water.

"A postcard from King City, California."

"Oh, Jesus! Jesus! Jesus! Oh, Jesus! Is he okay?!"

"Haven't seen him since he left home."

"What the hell does the postcard say?"

"It's blank."

"Blank? How do you know it's Othello?" She sucked off Jim Beam. Began to cry.

"I'm sorry, Mrs. Bolen. I received the first one—"

"When?!" she screeched.

"Seventy-eight," I whispered.

"Three goddamn years! Goddamn you, Mike! I'm his mother! God!" Jim clanked against something.

"I didn't want you to have to lie to the police."

"I'll lie to those bastards every holy day on the calendar."

I laughed. She sniffled, laughed through tears.

"Find him, Mike! And when you do, call me immediately.

Tell him to contact me through his grandmother in Havana, Illinois."

"Okay."

"Mike, I'm sorry, what I said. You boys drive a woman to fits!"

"I know."

"God bless you, Mike." She hung up.

12

September '81. I'd sweated in San Diego *dos años*. D hopped a bus to Suckerpunch. Bastard would be back. I mused about Scout. His postcard churned my legs. Hatched to hitch to King City. My Xanadu, deep six. I'd chewed enough off of her anyway. Tired of the stink. The noise. The murders. Tired of heroes. Neurotics. Addicts. I continued to slave sporadically as a construction laborer. Tangled with surfer girls. Jingled blood-bank ducats. Lived on Zingaro sandwiches and beans. Herradura. I moved into a Mount Helix house that looked like a spaceship. A friend, Joe "Mr. Natural" Dye, rented the UFO. Joe was a dwarf, three feet seven inches of beatific sweetness. He handed me a gypsy pass. My bedroom was separate from the main house, in the wing off the pool area, with a door to the outside. I dug the place. It had a boomerang roof. Illuminated starbursts lined the driveway.

Mr. Natural strolled Helix with phony credit cards pinned to his polar bear smoking jacket. Swilling gin and tonics. Redheads. He owned a wheatgrass gold mine—racks of trays stacked in the garage and a shed. Enough to sod a baseball field! UFO's vitals: Tailfin walls. Waterbeds. Plastic passed-out friends. Safari Extra Wildebeest room. Donovan lava lamp shrine. Tiki room—AKA "Coconut Drool"—where a barn owl crapped on the ready-to-ship cash crop.

Hitched San Diego County—to see what would spin out there, who I'd meet. Whirlygig Helix to beaches to Gaslamp Quarter saloons.

October. A red-wind Friday. The moon puffed angel dust. Stars dripped. Frothy sheepdogs humped next door. Mrs. Alvaras picked onions in Rubbermaid pants. Nipple clamps. The mister slithered on all fours, imitating a grunion. I sat in the kitchen over a Bud tall boy. Peanut M&M's. A car pulled up. Doorbell rang. I opened it. What? Othello? Othello! My once stalwart confederate! Emaciated! Chalky! Slicked macaw-blue hair! Bugging like a meth addict! King Tut's choker around his skinny neck. His eyes vibrated over me, unsurprised. He barged in toting a two-tone tan suitcase.

I stood there holding the door. Dumb. Excited. Scared. "Shut it, Mike," he popped.

My eyes strangled him. Scout shimmied. Sweated shoe polish. He scanned my place for cold tablets. Battery acid. A cliff. I peered outside. No posse. No hounds. I shut the door. Hugged my friend. His bad breath, BO—more telltale signs of a tweaker. I stepped back. Eyed his small suitcase.

"Where'd you pick that up? The drug dealer five-and-dime?"

"Yeah!" he shot back. "This, too," and reached behind his tangerine tank top. Pulled out a Colt .357.

"Stuck my dick in a hole that big last week."

Scout shook, giggled. Undulated like a caged cobra.

"Sit down," I commanded.

I sat on a stool at the kitchen bar. Scout sat down across from me. Set his suitcase on the counter between us. I poured shots of Old Crow.

"How'd you—?"

"Your dad. "Said you were coming to King City."

"I was."

He fired a nervous smile. The feds are on my trail, Mike! Genie sang the whole song. Pitch-perfect! Now I'm an FBI poster boy!"

"You ran. As good as pleading guilty. What the fuck did you expect?"

"I should have turned myself in, spilled? Given you up, too?"

"No!"

"Then what?"

"Nothing. Jesus. I would've done the same thing."

I leaned over the bar. Studied his suitcase.

"Keep it for me, okay? You're the only one I trust."

I went out to my bedroom, eased back into the kitchen, and stood over Scout. Dropped the murdered New Mexico girl's ID on the bar in front of him.

"Oh, Maria!" he wailed. "Where the hell did you get this?"

"Kill her?"

"What? No!"

"Atomic Al claims he found it in your fuck shack. He gave it to me because he didn't think you—"

"I didn't—!"

"Stab her? Come here for a trifecta?"

Scout laid his blue clown mop on the bar. He blubbered and squealed. I took the Crow by the neck. Stood it on its head. Boy came around a minute later.

"I'd been seeing her a month—more. We got stoned one night. I told her the Shriner's tale." He banged his fists. "She said I owed a debt to society. To Howard's family. That I never should have run. That I should turn myself in. I—I—I—"

"Uh-huh."

"Atomic or one of his pets did a Kojak. Think I know who. One of Al's employees—a local kid named Johnny Sample. A slimy carp! A real jealous fuck! He wanted to play king of the hill. We brawled a week after I got there. I busted his lip. Broke his nose. He fell off the hill. The other monkeys began to make fun of him. He vowed revenge."

"Why'd you brawl?"

"He called me out in front of Al's entire crew during lunch

break when Al wasn't around. I obliged the fucker. Then a week later I caught him sweet talking Maria the first time I brought her by Atomic's. I'd just come back from running an errand and this prick's got his fucking arm around her! A week later Maria's telling me he somehow got her number. Began calling her every day. Something was wrong with this guy, Mike. Know what I mean? You can tell when a guy's twisted. He killed her. I know he did. Then he framed me by planting her ID in my bunk." Scout's gaze bore into my eyes, pleaded, "Does my tune sound off-key, Mike?"

I leaned back, tore a wing off the Crow. Scout's gaze spun impatiently.

"No, kid, your tune isn't off-key," I purred, not entirely convinced. Tweakers made great liars.

Scout picked up Maria Sanchez's ID. Pinched her cheeks. Moaned. I slid the Crow into the monsoon. He gulped it. He sputtered a Guy Smiley. Squeezed my hand. "Our pact, remember? Blood brothers till the end."

"Always." I cocked a sucker punch: "Talked to your ma?"

"Hell, no! Keep the case for a while?"

I x-rayed the case again. "How long?"

"Until I change my hat. I'll find you, okay?"

"Where you staying?"

"Cemetery."

"I know people in Baja. You could hop down there."

Othello popped up. Hugged me. Looked at the suitcase. Daggered my eyes with a weak smile. "Don't wear any of my clothes, Mike. They're not clean."

He bolted out the front door. I ran after him. Watched him peel away. Thought of that Pig's Eye alley five years before. Poor Howard's bleeder. Poor, gallant Othello defending us! Scout at ten. Riding Glen Lake rainbows on his Sting-Ray. A tear slipped. Didn't know who I was crying for. Picked up the bottle. Took a belt of blackbird. Set the three-to-five stretch on the bar. Popped it. General Grant! Smelling like Palermo Christmas! Clams for Carmen! Counted the beat-up cross-eyed generals. Seventy-five grand! I stashed the suitcase in the hall closet. Lit a stogie.

Smooched Crow another hour.

A noise from the door to the pool, the direction of my BR. Spun around. Mrs. Bolen leaned against the doorjamb wiggling her hips. Frenchy fur had been in Cal three weeks now—two weeks before she showed at the UFO. She'd hired a King City private dick to bloodhound Othello. The St. Paul DA had promised a reduced sentence, manslaughter. Three years tops. Sure. I knew Othello wouldn't buy in. His words rang in my ear, "I'll never turn myself in! I'd rather be dead than do a stretch in the workhouse!"

For the past week, Flo'd shaken her ass on the roof. In the garden. In the dog kennel! Now she stood there hot as Angie Dickinson in *Big Bad Mama*. Crotchless panties. Sheer bra. Hula-Hoop hips. Phony tits. Forty-three years old. Twenty of it rope burns and fucking the mailman. Dyna-Flo yawned, grinned a Valium grin. She had been in dreamland during Othello's scene. A half-empty bottle of Chablis sweated against her thigh.

"Wanna loop-the-loop?" she shrieked, laughing. Grape ran down her leg.

"Dyna-Flo," I chuckled.

"Worn out, Michael?" she needled. Pounced.

We toasted Kamikazes! Kama Sutra! Kit-Kats! Slid the lily on kitchen counter. John Philip Sousa appeared in living room with marching band. Chimpanzees! We uncoupled. Gazed.

"Play it, Johnny, goddamn it!" Flo screamed.

Sousa hopped to. Petted his greasy beard. Pinched the medals on his chest. Waved his fat arms. The boys blew "The Stars and Stripes Forever."

Flo chorus-kicked, cried, "Bless you, Froggy Teddy Eddie Roosevelt!"

Sousa winked. Dyna-Flo curtsied. Flung her bra. We fucked on the Ping-Pong table. In the Safari Room. In the Hee-Haw Room. Donovan lava lamp crescendo. We coked up. Drained the bottle of Chablis. Ate Valium. Crashed around two. Fried steaks for a week before Flo flew fairies back to Frogtown.

I never chirped about Scout's visit or the murdered New Mexico girl. Did I feel guilty about holding out on Flo? Othello? No. I jittered about my Tom Sawyer. Our blood pact was the only sure thing I had. I'd go the distance with him no matter what. But the suitcase of Grants got hotter by the hour! I waited for the King City gumshoe, but the root canal never showed. Was he too cheap? Or still woozy from Flo's fluffs? Maybe Dyna-Flo had called him off. Maybe she figured her interrogation methods would work on me, make it rain—and if it didn't rain, there was nothing more to know.

13

A week gassed. Sigmoid agents beamed aboard. Sara Lee and Mr. Shinebox. A Turtle Cream Pie and a Nazi. I shook in the Purina kennel out back of the UFO. Fleas. Hairballs. Meter reader lady's panties hung on a nail next to Flo's. Mr. Natural pricked in a silk periwinkle kimono and Hiroshima slippers. Greeted the FBI with a highball and a hard-on. I snuck to the window. They had him on the hibachi! An hour on each side. Sweet-and-sour sauce. Mojo powder! Sara Lee flaunted her sexy gams. Mugs of Othello and me! Mr. Natural lost his pluck! Shinebox blistered. Brandished police photos of the Shriner!

Poor Howard's dead and gone. Pretty li'l girl with a red dress on. Sweat seeped through Mr. Natural's kimono. He teetered! Shinebox dropped another bomb! Black-and-whites of the New Mexico girl! Elvira makeup! Tarantula shawl! Sara Lee made Joe play Twister! Liar's Poker! But he didn't give me up!

The FBI cut out at seven p.m. I ducked into my room. Crammed the few clothes and belongings I owned into a Mr. Lucky cigar box. Waited for the onslaught. Footsteps! My door burst open. Mr. Natural blew in. Smoky. Dripping with Teriyaki.

"You've got an hour to vamoose," he growled and clomped out.

Othello's suitcase! The closet door glowed red! Mr. Natural had elephant guns! Deep-sea lawyers! VFW box tops! I feared the kimono would get a whiff of the moola. But he didn't! I peeled James T. Kirk. Phaser. Spock glow-in-the-dark boxers. Threw on flip-flops. Surf shorts. Grabbed Ulysses. Heavy as a warden's smirk. Mr. Natural bird-dogged. Watched me waltz down Lorena Lane.

"Palomino Club!" Grant pounded and screamed. "Whores for a month! Rosarito, you boob!"

"Not now," I muttered.

Lugged fat boy half a mile. Highway 8 West on-ramp. Wiggled my thumb. Orange Karmann Ghia spit flames. I ran to the window. *Ebony* cover boy. Nerf fro. Tight black T-shirt. Jalapeno hot pants. Gilded cowboy boots.

"Going near the Sports Arena," he said and toyed with a Zimbabwe earring. "You?"

"Beach."

"Well, lucky you. And if you're nice, I might just take you all the way."

Stuffed Grant behind the passenger seat. Climbed in. Cowboy ground first. Eased Karmann down the ramp. Pushed in Al Green cassette. "She kick you out?"

"Yeah."

"Too bad. Helix is nice."

"You don't live there?"

He laughed. "Ever seen a nigger in Helix?"

"No."

"Did a freelance gig. A b-day party for a divorcée."

"Oh, okay."

"What's in the case, blondie?"

"Seventy-five thou."

He barked. Rubbed his fro.

"Just kidding. Just some stuff."

"Uh-huh," he giggled excitedly, eyes rolling slot machine. Stopped at two lemons and a turd. "Know any hit men?"

"What? No."

"Want to put my boss down. Runs a titty club on Midway. The Condor. Ever been?"

"No."

Cowboy rolled out a victorious smile. "Quitting tonight." His face fell south again. "Been doing Ladies Night there for a few months. Tonight's my last gig. I'm going to get my paycheck, and then I'm gone."

He cranked Al. Lit a Viceroy. "Prick made me do things," he said under his breath. "Before he'd hire me." He dragged. Blew fire. "Only been doing it to pay my tuition at SDSU."

Grant licked my ear, murmured, "Give him some skins, asshole." Al Green poured warm honey down my shorts.

"What do you think about coming to the club with me?" Cowboy asked as we passed the 805 turnoff.

"I don't—"

"Lots of white bitches there," he smiled. "After my gig we could scoop up a pair. Nibble cocktails somewhere."

"Thanks, but I'm all in."

"Think about it, okay?"

Cowboy glided the Morena Boulevard exit a tune later. "I need gas," he said. Streaked into a Shell station on Napa.

I played full-service jock. Grabbed a squeegee and lathered the windshield while Cowboy pumped high-test. Eyeballs looped his get-up. I soaped the rear window. Hawked inside for a candy rack. Then I heard the Karmann's door slam! Ignition! Cowboy sped away. The gas hose fell out—petrol spewing. I bolted after him. He ran the light. Horns! Crash! Crunch! A beer truck slammed the Karmann. Chewed Cowboy up and spit him out the passenger door. The trucker bounced out, walked toward the crumpled Orange Crush can. Leaned over the morgue ticket. I slipped to the Karmann's driver's side. Bent in through the busted window. Rescued Grant. Sprinted across Friar's Road. Slid down an embankment of ice plant. Cut into the business park. Crouched behind Dumpsters. Sirens! Waited an hour. No hounds. Walked two blocks north on Savannah. Past blown-up abortion clinics. Swabbie tattoo parlors. Mexicans mooning in their lowriders. Pay phone on Naples, outside Twelve Step Liquor. Sign's small print read "If you're going to fall off the wagon, why not do it here?"

I pulled out my address book. Eyed Mermaid Mary's digits. She was a flush old cake-eater I'd met at a Caravaggio show—fondue after party. We hit it off for two reasons: a shared passion for Renaissance art and high-grade weed. Mermaid was a Five-O beach queen. Miss Whitebread 1944 (Pasadena) when she was eighteen. Swami's longboard champ two years later. Poor orange picker's princess. Lassoed by Nephtali Aaron. She'd told me he'd invented Valium. Sure. And then the Devil shoved him off the Woolworth Building. That I believed. Mermaid was the only person I could trust with Grant. Seventy-five K was something she smeared on a cracker. Dropped coin.

"Hello."

"Mermaid, it's Mike."

"Gummy Bear! How are you?"

"On the lam."

"Really? Are you all right?"

"Come get me?"

"Oh, my! Where?"

"Morena District."

"Okay!"

I rattled off directions. "You'll see a B-movie liquor store. I'll be Frenching the pay phone."

"Okay!" she laughed. "I'll be in the Jag. Twenty minutes."

Fucked the dog under a Blow-Pop tree. Gagged Grant. Picked glass, soft tissue out of his beard. Mermaid's white '58 Mark IX pomped the parking lot. Oh, bonita Mary! Punks out front stopped to gawk, expecting Keith Richards to hop out for junk, a fifth of Jack.

I slid out of the shadows. Flashed lion teeth at the punks. Tossed Grant into the back seat. Got in. Eyed Mermaid. She was paint-smeared. Bouffant. Pearls. XL Rams jersey covered her bare legs. She was a haiku. Doctor Zhivago's Lara. She blinked her sad Russian eyes. Smiled. Flicked open a monogrammed alabaster cig case. Plucked a machine-rolled Trainwreck J. Lit up.

Passed it. Ten dummy miles up 5. Exited at La Jolla Village Drive. Passed UC San Diego to La Jolla Farms Road. Mermaid ran her silver rings through her bleach job. I wondered what her digs looked like. We'd hung out several times, always at Pacific Beach or one of the nearby clubs.

"Welcome to the fattest little oyster in the nation. An enclave of blue bloods, celebs, artisans, and Jew haters."

"Huh?"

"Poor Nephtali wanted to buy here after we met in '51," she said as we glided past ten-million-dollar estates crowning Black's Beach. "But Jews weren't allowed to purchase homes anywhere in La Jolla until the early '60s. The transplanted Hitler Youth, AKA the city fathers, had to bend, or UC wouldn't have roosted here and begun laying golden eggs. Greed trumped anti-Semitism! Oh, Jesus! Sometimes I wonder why I stay here!"

Mermaid sailed the curving drive. It was inlaid with Gentiles! Panamanian slaves' skulls! She parked the truffle in front of a Gaudi castle. Eased out of the Jag. She looked at me inquisitively. Studied my suitcase. "But I do adore this house!"

"Uh-huh."

Gazed up. Baroque pinnacles. Adorned with Pharisees. Mackerel. Lynched lobbyists. We click-clacked over the drawbridge. Caracoled through the catacombs passing the J. Burst into the Czarina's lair. Smelled of Spartan semen. Clorox. Dali. I hawked around. Two Rothkos. A Jasper John. Four-foot crystal bong. Center stage, the rump of a canvas on an easel. Mermaid led me to a rhino sofa in front of the picture window. I sat. Plunked Grant. Gaped at the canvas. It was Toulouse-Lautrec. Absinthe grin. Ten-foot legs. Tuba penis.

"Like it?"

"Marvelous," I lied. "The bong?"

"That? A gift from George Harrison," she said wearily. "Germany. Hand-blown. Gold and ruby inset. This was our entertainment room. Before Nephtali . . ." Her voice faded.

"Been painting long?"

"Since my third nervous breakdown," she said quickly. "You

look drago, daddy. Sustenance?"

"Sure."

Mermaid zeroed. I hit the J. She soon misted again. Naked! Renoir bosom. Shaved cunt humming over tanned dolphins. Fiends inside me cavorted! Strapped on fleshy bayonets. Toulouse flashed his canines. Clawed his tuba.

"Mermaid!" I laughed in shock, coughing a gold nebula.

She fluttered to the Dali table. Plunked down a turtle-shell tray and exulted, "I'm a nudist! I'm always nude at home." She spread her arms, twirled. "Try it! It's liberating!"

I laughed and continued to drool.

"Does my vagina intimidate you?"

"Is it supposed to?"

Mermaid pranced within petting distance. "I just had a twat tuck. Like it?"

"Nice. Tongue-and-groove?"

She shrieked with laughter. "Dr. Mole gave me a sixteen-year-old's vagina to go with my youthful-looking breasts. I'm triangulated now."

"What did the sixteen-year-old get?" I asked rhetorically. I dropped trou.

Mermaid giggled with satisfaction. Ran her orbs over my shanks. Sat next to me. Eyed the case again. "Let me guess: Dirty shirts?"

"Seventy-five," I said and tore into a crab sandwich.

"Need a Mexican dry cleaner?"

"Know any?"

"They'll want ten."

"Keep it here after it's dropped off?"

"Certainly. How long?"

"A moon."

She froze. Grinned Mater Dolorosa. "What happened in Morena?"

"A tomcat tried to swipe the shirts. Got himself dinged up."

"Oh, dear! Hurt bad?"

"Not really. I told him what was in the case. He flunked the test."

"Flunked the test?" she brayed, shot up, and pinched her hips.

"That's not at all like you Michael. And your grade, professor?"

"D or D-minus."

"You get an F." She crossed her arms. Vaunted her tits. Gazed around the room.

"I know. I screwed the pooch."

She gave me a forgiving smile. "What do you think of the place?"

"It's something."

"Oh, we threw some wild wingdings here! The pool filled with Mumm's. One time, caviar."

"Caviar?"

"Blueberries. But, everyone was so blotto they didn't care if they came out dyed blue. Sinatra! Elvis! The Beach Boys! Nixon, that Jew hater, had the nerve to show up uninvited after Nephtali donated five mil to the Scripps Institute. Dicky was scrounging for his '72 re-election. In front of a crowd of Hollywood stars and socialites, Nephtali scribbled him a check for five dollars. Everybody laughed, thinking it was a joke! Oh, the utterly defeated and pathetic look on Nixon's face was priceless!" she crowed, raised her mitts, skipped around, stopping near Lautrec.

"The fountain of youth," she deadpanned. "Do you believe in such legends?"

"Like to."

Mermaid pulled a polished green stone out of her pussy! I looked on in shock. She held it up. "Amazonite!" she gushed. "A healing crystal! Like an antenna that transfers energy!"

"Cartoon Channel?"

Her jowls fell. But she quickly bloomed again. Pipped, "My feng shui guru, Master Chin, selected it. I carry it in my vaginal canal eight hours a day. It increases my chi and—"

"Chi?"

"Universal energy. Life energy ebbing in our bodies. Master Chin said I need to get feng shui aligned correctly to allow maximum chi. Would you mind assisting?"

"Promise I won't need rubber gloves."

She giggled. Tied a bandana around her forehead. Slipped the green stone underneath. "This is my third eye chakra," she whispered. She clamped a clothespin on each nipple. "These clothespins are from a meteorite. They conduct chi, too. Now I'm double triangulated! My third eye chakra and my meteorite breasts. And my breasts and my new vagina!"

"Jesus fuck," I whispered.

"Come on!" She skipped out the rear glass door.

I slogged after her. Goofball moon. Black pool the shape of a neuroses pill. Tongue depressor diving board. Six-by-six-foot sandbox.

"Who's the sandbox for? Grandkids?"

"Oh, I poop outside now!" she yelled over her shoulder as she stopped on an overgrown putting green at the cliff's edge. "I'm trying to reconnect with the earth mother."

I waded blue grass and gazed out at the majestic ocean as I approached Mary, who faced the brine. I stood next to her. She squeezed my hand, sucked sea air and giggled, "Chant with me, Michael! Pranava om!"

"Pranava om!" I moaned, trying not to laugh.

"Oooh! I'm surging!" she bellowed and squeezed my hand tighter. "Feel it, Gummy? Queen Califia! Amazonia! Our auras! They're melding!"

The only thing I felt was my prick twitch. It pig knuckled. Frosty moon rays swept Mary up onto a Greek pedestal. Twenty years peeled away. She gyrated! Collapsed!

"I'm ridiculous!" she cried. "Really fucking ridiculous! I know! Oh, god!" She pulled the shades.

I scooped up the crumpled queen. Found her Liberace boudoir and dumped her there. Unclamped the meteors from her tits. Wrestled with myself on the rhino sofa. Jacked off. Zeed.

Mermaid awoke as Doris Day. Naked. Vaselined. Humming "Que Sera, Sera." The previous night's channel a test pattern. I followed her to the garage. Vintage motorcycles! Coupes!

"Whichever you like," she sang.

I mounted a '41 Indian 4. Maroon and white. Fan fenders. General Custer saddle. Femur handlebars. Fired it up. Kissed Mermaid's cheek.

"A friend named Othello may call about the money," I said.

"It's his. Please let him have it whenever he wants it."

"Okay." She donned a look of concern. "You going to be all right, Mike?"

"Yeah. Thanks."

"Shirts in a month!" she yelled and waved as I roared out of the cave.

14

I needed a place to flop. Churned south along the beach toward Olive Oil's. I'd swayed at the surfer girl's Mission Beach tiki shack on and off. We'd met on a sunspot. First date had lasted three days.

Twenty minutes shook. Then Mission Beach. Oases for reptiles. Flimflams. Pedophiles. Rolled past seraphim passing out religious tracts. Coke bunnies. Junkies sucking dick under the Giant Dipper. Midget jugglers. Tourists ogling bodybuilders.

Parked on the corner of Fruity Pebbles and Rod Serling. Junior Republicans strolled past wearing the uniform: Vuarnets. Lacoste shirts. Prosthetic septums. I chewed the payphone receiver outside Zebra Mating Station. Dropped ducats. Olive Oil gave me the high sign. I squeezed inside Zebra's womb. Full of sunflower surfers and two-bit grifters. Dead bodies fell out of the TV above the cash register. Bought a pound of Truman Capote. Box of rubbers. Scratch off wet dream. Kicked the Indian. Spun right on Narcissist Avenue and parked. Olive, pulsing in a red bikini, waited on her porch.

After a week of lies and Johnny Carson, I left Olive's. Worked the jackhammer. Gypsied on a half dozen couches from Pacific Beach to Ocean Beach. Mermaid phoned a month later. The shirts were clean. Rode the Indian to La Jolla. Groped Ben Franklin. Sixty-five grand. Dapper and spiffy! Hugged naked Mermaid. Took ten shirts. All for Othello. Mermaid let me stash the rest of Scout's bundle in her safe. I didn't have anyplace else to hide it. I hadn't heard from Othello. I didn't tramp to King City—he wouldn't go back there with hounds on his trail. Was he dead? In jail? That's a lot of loot to leave behind. I feared the worst. It was time to find him!

But six moons seared with no smoke signals from Scout. Then, mid-July 1982, a blank postcard in my Mission Beach PO box, forwarded from the Helix UFO. Finally! Ho, Scout! My cousin. My killer. The latest card was a lithograph of a clown: "Dillon and Sons Amusement. Greatest Show in the West!" Long Beach postmark. June. I flipped the card over. In fine print along its bottom edge was the circus's summer schedule: Salinas and Santa Cruz this week. Santa Rosa, Yuba City the next. All underlined in pen. Thunderbolts. Greasy psalms. Scout had joined the circus!

I was hot to lasso my Tom Sawyer. I pined for a long ramble. Penicillin. New skin. Sick of Crayola patriots—idols!—crucifixions!—the quest for fame! Chewing on that rotted my teeth. How to get back to the savanna? Stumbling naked with a spear. Calloused. Misty. Vicious as spring!

The Flynn brothers' shack in OB was my duck at the time. The Flynns. Bostonian. Ophidian. Dionysian. My shamrock brothers! Coke on the kitchen table. Saint Mary on the wall. 30.06 Browning behind the front door. Rock 'n' roll records strewn everywhere. I'd met Frank Flynn tumbling in a plaster mixer. Twenty-five. Punk. Patriarchal. Wore horns for strangers. Threw moxie Dempsey jabs. Proud of his tight ass and Polaroids of naked girlfriends.

Henry Flynn. Ex-marine. Lanky. Aw, shucks. Applesauce and animal crackers. Rolled joints and women like a gentleman. On a corned-beef-and-cabbage Saturday I stuffed supplies into a Kelty rucksack in the Flynns' rumpus room. The night before, I'd sewn Othello's ten K into a secret rabbit hole inside the pack. Didn't peep a word about the green or Othello to the Flynns or anybody.

Frank slid out of the bedroom. Crinkled boxers. Hungover like St. Patrick's Day parade pissing drizzle. Rubbed his rooster comb. "Today, Mike?" he crowed Boston.

"Uh-huh."

Frank rolled his eyes at Henry, who'd poked his head out of the kitchen. Bacon and eggs wafted. Henry chuckled, gave Frank a look that said, *Don't worry. This dope will be back in a few days*.

"Fucking pogues," I muttered playfully.

"Goddamn straight!" boasted Frank. "Blood green as clover! Green as JFK's! Gene Kelly's! No part shylock, frog, Rhine monkey. Aren't you part wop, Mike?"

I laughed. Continued packing.

Henry popped back out. "How long you going to be?" he asked with an airy smile.

"A month. More."

They snickered.

"Hitchhike for a fucking month?" bellowed Frank. "Where the hell you going to go?"

"Somewhere over the rainbow."

"Why don't you take Dimples in the back room and go somewhere over the rainbooowww?" he sang mockingly. "She's in my bedrooooooom!"

"Nah," I said.

Night before I'd heard the paddies pulling prizes out of Dimples. She was girlish. Poodle. Petite. A connoisseur of phalluses and cunts. Living the life of Sappho. In public, wholesome as milk and Oreos.

Frank hovered over me. "Where you going?"

"Tibet. Heard they sell horse sense there."

"Horse shit, in spades. Hey, you can be our guru. Get a load of this guy, Henry."

"Lovely," Henry spouted from the kitchen, bubbled to the

doorway, leaned against paint.

"Where you going to sleep?" Frank moaned, drifted away.

"In horse shit."

They laughed.

Dimples appeared in a beige nightie. She was a half-empty fifth of sherry, cig butts floating in the foam, greasy palm prints all over the bottle. She squatted at the end of the table. Stuck her thumb in her mouth. Flashed her signature "Who me?" look. Frank glared at me. Jerked his horns toward the back room. I shook my head.

"Really, Mike. How far you going?" asked Henry.

"Up the coast. Northern Cal, Oregon, Washington, and—"

"Take the choo-choo," pleaded Frank. "No money? He's a hopeless gypsy, Henry. What are we going to do? We know you get off on thumbing. That's cool. Jumping into the hippie-yippie experiential soup pot. The oneness with the universal mind. The fucking danger. Hitching around town, I'll buy that." He lit a Marlboro, dragged to the burn ward, blew ligatures at Dimples, whispered with disbelief, "Washington?"

"Frank's scared for me?"

"A fucking genius, Henry."

"Ever hitchhiked?"

"Once. You forget? I told you last Easter after you threw up on Connie the Queen. Flat tire on the Jersey Turnpike. I got robbed. How much money you got?" he barked, tugged his pecker, barged over.

"Twenty bucks," I said, wishing I'd said, "Enough."

"Jesus Christ!" he bellowed. "Henry!"

Henry jibbed into the bedroom. Returned to hand me three Jacksons. Dropped into the recliner next to me.

"Thanks," I said, pocketed Jackson. Guilt grabbed a claw hammer.

Frank picked up my supply list. "Henry, get a load of this!" he mugged. "Ready List—for a Michigan wop: Dog bones (three), AK-47, cartridges, rubbuz!"

"Rubbers!" Henry snorted, shrieked. Dimples tittered.

"A pork chop. A knife. Free coupon to any California VD

clinic good to December thirty-first. Cigars. Grenades!"

"Cute, for an asshole who's never camped," I sassed.

Henry gave a thumbs up. Dimples giggled. Flashed pussy. Frank soured.

"What about all the fucking nuts running around?" he asked.

I flipped him off.

Frank relit his Marb. Dragged. Pointed it at me like a pistol. "The Southside Strangler killed another one last week in LA and—"

"Frank! Jesus!" scolded Henry.

"What!" shouted Frank.

"I'm going," I said.

"Wait!" pleaded Henry.

He breezed to the phonograph. Spun the Doors' first LP. We threw arms around each other's shoulders, like at many record parties before, and sang along.

Frank gagged the Doors after "Soul Kitchen." Stuck another butt in his teeth. Crossed his arms across his chest. Shook his potato head. Smiled and yawped, "Hot shit! Fucking all right! Don't be an asshole. Call if you run into trouble."

"Sure."

I zipped the Kelty. Forty Swisher Sweet cigarillos. Zippo. A vial of Boris Karloff with an eye dropper. A Buck knife. A map of California. A can of Dinty Moore Beef Stew. A jug of water. A leftover pork chop from Grandma's OB Café. All three postcards from my Tom Sawyer.

15

Fled OB at noon. Rough and ready! Humming *Song of Roland*.
On the lookout for lightning. Mayhem. Bull fairies. The sun
spit butterflies. I glided down Muir Street. A winged quail.
Knew what I was: A pilgrim in a B Western. Surrounded by vil-
lains. Whores. Conquistadors. Sons of slave owners. Indian
killers. Old Faithful pissing hubris. Bad men sat around the
ranch—eating all the pie and ice cream. Needed to shed my
pocked hide. The pus of saints. Until I was a lean, true bullet.
Hitchhiking was a waning art. The new arts: Serial killing. Para-
noia. Helium Bibles. Leaders in purple robes guzzled Miracle-
Gro. Spewed angels' piss. Swung cats against tree trunks after
the show. Time cut into me!—gorged marrow! This was my
chance! Othello's circus would be in Salinas for two days. It was
a long stroll—425 miles—but I was primed to make it. A stop
along the way to ogle the old dames of the LA theater district.
Vaudeville! Talkies! Baroque bastions of WWII escapism!
  Washed three blocks to Jimmy's Liquor. Blinking orange
paisley. Highway 8's vulva. The anointed highway! Smelling like

my fourth grade teacher, Mrs. Mackie!—ambrosial!—wicked! Eight was a beacon for back-East runaways. Derelicts. Fools of the western dream. Arias swirled inside me! Of victory! Vivacity! Exotica! Immaculate as starlings. But then the starlings plummeted! Shrieking! D—the hawk of my affliction—rose up! Torching fires along the Apollonian shores. D summoned blowflies! Thousands! Laying larvae in children's cadavers. Sirens! Bullhorns! "Pssht! Give up! Pssht!" I'd always been afraid. Perverted. Pursued by D's he-men. She-men. G-men. Fuck that! I'd fight the ruffians off for good this time! Knock 'em dead!

I flashed my thumb. Strangled thirty minutes. Pulled out a notebook and marker. Wrote "Mars," big and black. Blazoned it. The first fella who saw it foot-fucked his brakes! My heart spun my legs! Ran to the Plymouth sedan. Genuflected! The door sprang open. Mute Mel—a Betty Crocker cake mix. German Chocolate. No milk. No eggs. He breathed through his skin. Flashed Morse code with his eyes. Taught "Taking Marx Seriously—the Rubber Didactic" at San Berdoo State. Sold see-through wetsuits and velvet Elvis paintings out of his trunk.

He dumped me on Highway 15 at Temecula—halfway to LA. I flipped the page in my notebook. Scribbled "Oz." The second lizard laid licorice! Zenith van popped portal. "Ed's Pest Control" splashed across its side. I hopped in. Zoom! L. Ron Hubbard disciple. Waxen. Wiry. Zion beard. Pinhole pupils. Tattoo of a human heart hovered above a volcano on his right biceps. Frowsy copy of *Dianetics* on the dash. Drano anthill sparkled on the cover.

"Oz? Are you a prophet?"

"Nah," I laughed. "Downtown LA?"

"The snake pit! Hairy! What for?"

"The old theater dis—"

"Incest! Secret mountain strongholds! Hieroglyphics!" he gushed. "We're preparing for the masters of sleep. Dianetics is as important as the discovery of fire! The revelations of the messiahs! The invention of the wheel!"

I shook my head in disgust. Moped out the window.

Lazarus flicked a Winston. Dabbed it in the cocaine. Sparked it. Blurted, "Know what you're thinking. Lies, all you've heard. L. Ron Hubbard's great works! Power spots! Snow White Program! Babylon Working! Hoity-toity goiter holy!"

I gazed at the headshot of his savior taped to the dash. "What's up with the huge knot on L. Ron's forehead?"

"His second brain!" he beamed. "He willed it! He claimed it! All future church members will have one!"

"L. Ron's a fucking madman."

Lazarus's pyramid-eye rays scorched. The Nile emptied! Mud smeared Cleopatra's tits. Straw-dog catcher pulled up to my window. Lazarus went Donnybrook. He screeched onto the shoulder near the next exit, where a sign read "Cope's Custom Slaughter—Adult Room."

I slapped the bricks. Rode the lava flow to the bottom of the ramp. Dusk. A ride later, downtown LA vomited, rolled over. A wrinkled broad with thin hair. A tattered, champagne-stained flapper. Smacking fish lips. Mumbling excuses. Skid Row wafted. I poured out of the Dodge Duster at Sixth and Broadway. The Palace Theatre groaned. A moldy cherry parfait. Garnished with sawed-off legs. Blue-collar Latinos lined in front of the box office. Crummy marquee read "King Kong starring Fay Wray." Pulled out my vial of Boris Karloff. Dropped ten thousand volts into each eye. A gurney squeaked out of the abandoned dry cleaner next door. A blue arm fell out from under the sheet. The crowd gaped. Murmured. I muscled in to get a look. The arm pointed a thousand miles away. Pointed across the street, where there was a premier at the Los Angeles Theatre. Crisscrossing searchlights. Tuxes and gowns. An ice wagon farted. Whizzing red lights. Squealed tires at the curb.

As the gurney slipped past Detective José El Lobo, he blew, "She's got her float in the Rose Parade now." He fussed with the mercury drain tubes sticking out of his neck and ribs. Took a hearty drag off his Amoeba. "Her motherfucking squatter's room looked like Saturday night on Skid Row," he moaned. Switched on his gamma-ray filter. "I bet the coroner finds the hearts of ten men underneath her fingernails when he scrapes her for aerosol and joy miners."

"You mean the balls of ten men, Chief?" cracked El Lobo's protégé, an Aqua Velva snipe in Florsheims.

"You're too young to be such a dick, kid."

Aqua smiled.

At the LA Theatre, a hightop limo pearled. Tuxes, gowns oohed, gasped. Doors contracted. Three wobblers popped up. Ten-foot heads!

"Oh, god!" a woman screamed. "He's my absolute favorite!"

Wobblers teetered! Zigzagged on the red carpet. Heavy heads bobbing. One fell. Head split open. Flying fish flew out! Sparrows! El Lobo pulled his rumble gun. Aqua followed. Waited. Sucking sounds! Gurgling! Six naked clones scurried out! Dripping cerebrospinal fluid. Two feet tall. Transparent red skin. Blue veins bulged underneath.

"Holy Moses! They look like baby robins!" a man called out.

"*Vámanos!*" commanded El Lobo. Throng veed.

Cops blasted. All six of the clones splattered. Everyone laughed and clapped.

"Where are my horses?! Where are my guns?!" wailed a high voice behind us.

Everybody spun around. A bearded ventriloquist bugged under the streetlight. Bogart trench coat. Hemiptera eyes. He groped a Charles Bukowski dummy in a baggy green suit. The dummy's legs shook. Mouth snapped open and shut.

"Goddamn scratch on an eight ball," muttered Aqua.

"Where are my motherfucking horses?" wailed Charles. "Get your guns and come west! Sirens from the desert. Nefarious invaders dancing on Malibu! Hee! Hee! Oily weddings. Jew stags crashed a Palestinian slumber party! Pledges of snake holes and rain. Inventing sin. Lost as a judge. The pomp! There's a door. Past indoctrination and piss! Where are my goddamned horses? Get your guns and come west!"

El Lobo shoved through the crush. Strode to the ventriloquist. "Here're your horses, amigo," he growled. Pulled his hellmaker out of its shoulder holster. Fired. Blew the dummy's head off. El Lobo twirled. Barked, "There'll be no inciting of violence or anarchy in any of the five appointed Hostile Districts!"

A loud humming noise spooked me.

"Hover train!" a woman shouted.

We all scattered. Tuxes and gowns looked on phlegmatically. Hover train descended. Stopped ten feet above the ground. I bolted into a defunct liquor store. Dove behind some boxes. Peeped out the window. The train's doors banged opened. A detail of Gravitron girls hopped out, scattering zithronium bugs. Like winged horseshoe crabs! Their blue thermal sensors gleamed. Zing! Zeng!

The ventriloquist darted inside. Crouched next to me. Plopped the Bukowski dummy down. Eyed my rucksack.

"Long walk?"

"Yeah. Salinas."

He torched a butt. Gave me one. Studied my eyes. Chuckled, "On the lizard?"

I cackled.

"Ooooo! I'm too goddamned old for any of that shit. I'll stick with the grape."

I scanned the scene outside the storefront. Blurry colors, lights, people streaked by. "What's all the fuss?"

He gazed out at the benign scene. Two rookie cops shot the shit. Picked at their snot. A lifer shooed away lookie-loos.

"Oh, don't worry, kid," he chuckled. "It's an immigration run."

Boris Karloff slapped my head, whispered in my ear, "He's a liar. The Gravitron girls are real. Puff queens hand-picked by the mayor for high scores on mandatory blood draw and Gold Citizens exam. You're not safe here."

"I heard about these immigration runs," I said to the ventriloquist, "but this is the first time I've—"

"A son of a bitch, huh?" he drawled. Fussed with his beard. Pulled on his bottle of Mad Dog.

I looked at him closely. "Charles Bukowski?"

"Sure, if you want me to be," he purred with a razor smile. "Like my little show?"

"Yeah," I said. He passed the Dog. I swilled.

"Well, I do what I can to cross up these damn new whatever

they call themselves. Guardian Angles or some shit."

I laughed.

"Far from the beach, aren't you, surfer boy?"

"I want inside the Palace or any of the other old girls. But, I'll wait until the Gravitron sisters leave."

"I was just funning with you before," he chuckled. "You're zilo. No one out there except a few coppers doing a mop job after an OD."

"Really?"

"They'll be sticking their cocks in donuts soon." He faded to black.

I peered out. Hover train! Parading lights. Crazy voices. Battle cries! Skinned the Mad Dog. I lay down on the floor. Hoped to zee until bacon and eggs. Not a chance. I was throbbing like Magneto Man after a Hasbro shake. Out the window, I could see the moon. A witch's eye! Hunting mice. Next to me, Bukowski was dreaming. I stole a cig. Waited. Heard terrible sucking sounds. Screams! Peered out. The sewer drains opened toothy jaws! Swallowed the hover train! The Gravitron girls! The blue boys! All vanished. Silence. I wandered out. Downtown LA at four a.m., a drowsy behemoth. Festering. Mad. Crawling with death. Wasted angels. I crept two blocks to Mister Donut. Bought bear claws. Grenades. Cyanide. Went back and fell asleep next to Bukowski at five.

Awoke at noon. He'd blown. I raked my hair. Waded through shit to the Los Angeles Theatre.

Notice on the swinger read "Available for Special Events Only."

I slapped a pickpocket. He slunk off empty-handed. The Palace's marquee winced like a junkie in sunlight. I knelt. Muttered a prayer. Stood. Slobbered on a Slim Jim. Plonked the Kelty down next to the flicker house's back door. Chevy Stepside blazed into the alley. Skidded to a stop. A white-haired man at the wheel. Bloody Mary complexion. He popped the octopus window. Flung open the door. Red polo shirt. No pants. Pecker stiff as a wooden Indian. He held the chief by the throat. Ran his balls north to south.

"Give you twenty dollars if you let me give you a blow job!"

he said.

I lifted my shirt. *Whitey, meet Mr. Shiny Buck.* He sped off. I twirled. Coughed up bottle rockets. Fingerfucked the Palace's back door. Sloppy lock! I slipped in. Stygian. Stumbled around the screen to the stage. Sparks flew! Lights! Pigs! Swine! In a thousand seats! Yorkshires! Irish Grazers! Choctaws! Sitting perfectly silent. Perfectly still. Staring at the milky screen through 3-D glasses—with flaming erections—ham sandwiches. I wondered! Quaked! Wedding cake walls. Gold-leaf murals—vaudeville's muses. Dance! Drama! Music! Song! Bouquets of lavender and Mr. Clean. The screen flared. *The Sound of Music's* opening credits rolled. I tried to run! Whirring sounds! I was siphoned inside the screen! Listerine-green fields! Tootsie-Pop tulips! Snow-cone Nazi Alps. Dead Jews hung from the firs! Bolsheviks trumpeted. Maria frolicked. A boy, two Boston terriers trailed behind her. I ran toward them.

Maria flapped her arms, sang the first lines of the title song.

The boy sniggled. Twirled. I got closer. It was Pop, at seven or eight! Maria couldn't see me. Pop could. He beamed while dancing around singing.

Then he giggled. "You're gonna die!"

"What?"

"Today!" he laughed. He scampered away. Dissolved.

I was in a dusky room. Pop knelt next to his bed. His ribs tuned a broken radio. He looked ten. Funeral Prayer sheet on the night table: "In Memory of Thomas Walsh." Pop's father. Pop cried out. I knelt. My eyes adjusted to the light in the humble room. I was pathetic! Imbecilic! The doctor's son had amounted to nothing! My eyes teared. Light flashed. Another room. Dusty. Fancy 1940s women's hats. Pop's ma, Ruth Walsh, crafted custom hats. The door squeaked. Pop! Fourteen or fifteen. Hair like crow's wings. Sweaty Bible. Plastic rosary. He hurled Jesus. The rosary followed. Sat at his mother's work bench. Gently, Pop took the feathered hat off the mannequin's head. A custom number ordered by a Blueberry Briar baroness. He brushed the dust off. Studied the skilled craftwork. Erupted into tears! I felt Pop's terror! I was a derelict! A sensualist! Destined to mop floors in a unicorn slaughter room! His fear stole my breath. I shook with it! The skinny Cortland orphan slammed his fists against his thighs.

Pop held up a pair of deuces! Screamed, "Is this all!" Hyperventilated. Collapsed!

Bright light. Flash! I was inside my favorite photo of Pop— a nine-year-old fatty watering tomatoes, 1942, Cortland, NY, victory garden. Flash! I was jettisoned onstage. I tumbled. Stood gangly. Palace aphotic. Deserted. Walked out into a school of bright, filthy LA carp.

16

Popeyed Dinty Moore. Blimpy limbs! Yuk! Yuk! Yuk! Watch out Bluto! Needed a shorty to 10 West on-ramp. Ten would get me to the Coast Highway, three hundred miles to Salinas! Scout's circus would be there for another day and then head north fifty miles to Santa Cruz. Winked ten fingers. VW bus rainbowed. Parrots fluttering in its wake. A Warhol paint job. Arcadian plates. The door creaked open. A Deadhead in a gas mask. WMC dreadlocks. Tie-dyed T. Crayfish trunks. Wooden leg.

"Huntington Beach," he muffled through the strawberry. "Uncle Jerry and the band tonight!"

"Northbound. Highway 10?"

"Right on, dude!"

Climbed into the cocoon. The apostle shifted into hummingbird. Pegged the throttle. The walls were frosted with Dead posters. Marmalade. FBI wanted pinups. Bean burrito wrappers. Van full of sprouting Chia pets. Black Lab pups chased hens over two Wookie girls crashed in a sleeping bag. Dreads. BO. Hairy legs. Incense wafted from a little urn.

"I'm Wham-O," the driver said.

"Tin Man. The mask?"

"GP-5. Soviet. My magnetron's out of whack. Positive ions have infiltrated my organs."

"Oh?"

"A simple yin-yang imbalance. Due mostly to not showering for a week. I try to live *in vivo*. Tonight, I'll shed these savage serotonin in the ocean. Get splashy splashy!"

"Uh-huh," I said with straightest face possible.

"I'm a hundred and thirty-two!"

"Huh?"

"It's my hundred-and-thirty-second Dead show."

"Really?"

"Ever been?"

"No."

With a look of disappointment, Wham-O jerked his dreads rearward, whispered, "My wives China and Dharma. Pulled an all-nighter after the Ojai show last night. Shakedown Street was a jumping. Sold nearly a hundred Chia pets! Bob Weir bought one! Want one? I'll throw in a pup for an extra ten-spot."

"Nah."

"Know what else?"

"Huh?" I said, scoping for a Highway 10 sign.

Wham-O lifted his gas mask. Stretched his catfish mouth, whooped, "Sixty-six more and we get a prize! A full Swiss-cheese fondue set, including a wig of blonde braids!"

"Wow!" I feigned firecrackers.

He pulled the mask down again. "Hear about the guy who tried to stop Reagan's campaign train?" he asked.

"No."

"It was me!" He tapped his wooden leg. "Ronnie's extraordinarily evil," he retched magnesium. "Has had sex with chimps and horses. Going to pluck the eagle!"

I laughed.

"Sorry. I'm still half-wasted from last night's show. Anyway, some call me the Anaheim Hero. I sat on the railroad tracks in protest. Train didn't even slow down! Dragged my leg clear to

Fresno." Wham-O grinned slyly. "Kicker is, I get nine hundred and three dollars a month social security! For life!"

I sat dumbfounded. The phony martyr tossed me at the Highway 10 ramp to Santa Monica.

17

I lit a Swisher. Chewed on Wham-O's Chiclets universe and chuckled. Took out Othello's circus postcard. Rubbed my hands over it. Fretted. I wondered what kind of job Scout had landed under the big top. If meth still stomped on him. If he'd zapped the New Mexico girl. Flipped open my notebook. Scrawled "Highway 1." The city bled. An hour blipped. A black limo slid lizard. An electric window whirred. The driver was an android! Black suit. Tie, hat. Herky-jerky.

"My destination is Santa Barbara," it said in gray monotone.

"You're not going to go *Blade Runner* on me or some shit, are you?"

"I don't understand the reference," it said. "I'm not familiar with *Blade Runner*, and I can't offer you any shit. However, there's a full bar of alcoholic beverages in the rear of the vehicle to assist in depressing your central nervous system."

"What are you called?"

"Timothy 3. A hybrid humanlike cyborg. Today, my creators are testing a new benevolence program. I'm limited to take you within a one-hundred-mile radius of greater Los Angeles. Would you like a lift, young man?"

I opened the back door. Flung the Kelty in and slid in after it. The machine swung its head around. Greased a creepshow smile. Turned back. Hit gas.

"We're ninety-seven miles from Santa Barbara," it reported. "We should reach our destination in approximately one hour and thirty-nine minutes, depending on weather and traffic conditions or possible death."

"Possible death?!"

"There's a 15 percent probability that an earthquake of significant magnitude will send us off the cliff into the Pacific Ocean. You will not survive such an event."

"Anything else?"

"There's a 32 percent probability that my driving skills are inadequate for this test mission."

"And I will not survive such an event."

"Affirmative."

I poured a Cutty Sark deuce. Threw it down. Shook out a Heineken.

"Say, Timothy, what else do you do besides drive poorly?"

"Racketeering. Embezzlement."

Othello's ten grand! "Who the hell have you stole from?"

"The Carlisle Robotics Company based in Los Angeles, California. Various companies in the Hollywood, California, entertainment industry that have granted me temporary employment."

I laughed. Half cowered. "How does it feel?"

"I possess no human feelings or emotional responses whatsoever. I was modeled after top Washington politicians."

I roared. Pounded Heineken.

"I have a confession to make," Timothy 3 said.

"What?"

"My creators are also testing a recently installed humor program. I've been having some fun with you. How am I doing?"

"Great," I said with relief.

"Thank you."

We skirted Santa Monica and got on Highway 1. Quixotic seascapes to Malibu. Oxnard. A hundred miles of Robert Frost poems. I snorted heifers. Eucalyptus. Monarchs. Was a phantom! A morgue attendant on holiday. Dissecting reptiles. At my destination every second. Every minute. Highway 1 turned into 101 as we entered Santa Barbara.

"Any special departure point?"

"Medicine store."

"A pharmacy?"

"Liquor store."

"I have downloaded your 'medicine store' reference into my slang files."

The machine pulled booze-smooze into Baba's north end, near Goleta. Kids pressed their tits against the lizard's smoked windows. Stammering for John Travolta. Olivia Newton John. I birthed. Hundred-dollar shoes slunk away, disappointed.

"Have a nice day," Timothy 3 said.

"Thanks for not getting me killed," I said jokingly.

"Maybe next time," it said and drove off.

I bought a quart of Bud. Ham on rye. Mounds Bar. Lice kit. Five p.m. Drowsy. Strolled the service road to the 101 on-ramp. Past a pear orchard. Bat phones. I shed the Kelty and leaned it against my thigh. A bevy of hobos drank whiskey in the shade along the RR tracks. Flies on a Monet canvas. Dressed in slop-brown Salvation Army suits. I gaped at the hobos. They were airy as angel food. Maybe they had it right? America's nomads! Five-and-dime geniuses! Aristocrats of filth! Unshackled from dogma. Institutions. Taboos. Ambitions. One of them, a sympathy card on chicken legs, stumbled toward me. Held out a cigarette.

"Going to Pioneer." He wheezed Boone's Farm. "You?"

"Salinas."

He handed me the butt.

"Thanks, pal," I said. Lit up.

He sparked one. Asked, "Salinas? What for?" He scratched his little beard, a sticky candy wrapper that'd fallen behind a sofa.

"See the circus," I said, looking him over. He was twenty-two, tops. His shirt a sack of wet gunpowder. Tumbleweed trousers. Let go of the throttle on the first turn.

"I rode an elephant once! Fell off. Why don't you tramp with me to Pioneer? It's not far from Tahoe. You can hit the casinos."

"No thanks." I saddled the Kelty. Snaked along the ramp. Sympathy Card caught up to me. "Name?"

"Sleepy."

"I'm Horace Greeley," he bellowed. Pointed at the other bums. "And over yonder is the Continental Congress. Sleepy, you want a new name? Grab one out of the sky and try it on." He eyed me up and down. "Davy Crockett! Hot damn, potatoes and gravy! Nice to meet you Davy!"

I smiled. Dragged on the cig. Envisioned Othello funning in his coonskin cap. Then the bloody Shriner!

"Jungle with us tonight, Davy," horsed Horace. "Bare-Knuckle Bill will be cooking up his special: Adam and Eve on a raft."

"No thanks. Heading out."

"Watch out if you don't get lucky. Saint Barbara's finest will chain you up three days for vagrancy."

"No shit?"

"Best find us, or truck a mile north to the city limits. They won't run you off there."

"Much obliged, Horace." I jaywalked to the service road. Pilfered a pair of prime pears. Crossed back. Floated up the ramp.

"We'll jungle in the orchard, Davy!" he called out. "You'll smell the smoke!"

Rambled north. Past the city limit. Lemon-meringue mansions. Par-three front lawns. Negro coachman statuettes. Coked-out jet setters barbecuing Mexicans out back. Another mile. Big trees. Twilight crept in. Milky streetlight illuminated the prize! A desolate, pearly '61 Continental! Sleeping in the toasted weeds against the bleached ribs of the Goleta Baptist Church. Suicide doors had been swung wide. Trunk and hood were debutantes with legs in the air. Undignified as a looted corpse. Snooped in the back seat. Clean as a hog's trough!

Tossed in the Kelty. Closed the trunk and sat on it. Gazed childlike at the dusky sky. Lit a Swisher off Venus. Washed down beef jerky, pear with Bud. No cops. Snoozed like the Seven Dwarfs!

18

My feet danced on Highway 1 a fart and a piss after the rooster. I pulled out my map. Two hundred twenty miles to Salinas. It was Othello's circus's last day there. I hoped to make it by night-fall. Scrawled "Steinbeck" on a piece of cardboard. Stuck it under my waistband. A Winnebago winked its brakes. Catfish on Sunday! The exalted door hissed open. Hoofed heartbeats to the Andromeda portal. I stood at attention at the threshold. Saluted the captain. Forty. White. Glasses. Conservative as a banker's desk. Xanadu in his smile.

Caked, "Welcome aboard!"

I jumped in. The captain eased the steamboat back into the current, up the river. I climbed three shaggy steps. Gawked at the cabin. It was a rolling mission! There were four other road-worn nomads riding! Turds on Wonder Bread! Sprinkled among three shiny kids. Twin pigtailed girls. Dime apiece. But-terscotch boy runt. An Aunt Bambi cradling a bambino rode shotgun. Bouffant. Buxom. Two-for-one soul. I was jolted. Why would they pick up hitchers? Hawking coupons to heaven?

"This is my wife, Maureen, with our newest edition, Ephraime," beamed Captain.

Bambi paraded bad teeth, tugged on the sleeve of her Washoe blouse. "Rest are ours, too."

"Hi," I said.

The girls smiled silver spoons. Giggled. Butterscotch bit into a peanut-butter-and-jelly sandwich. Flipped down his Yosemite Sam mask. Hopped around imitating the volatile bastard.

"Find a seat!" barked Captain.

I plunked down between two gypsies sitting at a round table. Spread with loaves of bread. Deli cuts. Cheese. Chips. 7UP. Wanderer on my right: Bottom of the eighth. Two outs. Silver-red beard. Durocher's Cubs cap. Violet suit blackened by a thousand boxcars. Guy on my left was half Durocher's age. Twice his size. Sad Tolstoy vodka face. Duct-taped sweater showed off his hairy toots. Bear gut. Opposite us, on a couch, a pierced angelina snored. A stick of dynamite in his teeth. His fly half-open. Next to him, a bad actor moped out the window. Thirty-five. Handsome. Slick clothes. Buzzing like a busted fluorescent light. A grifter? A runner? The kids didn't go near him. Durocher and Tolstoy glanced up at me over triple-decker sandwiches.

"How long you been tramping the ribbon?" I asked Durocher.

"Civil War!" he cried out.

Everybody shrieked with laughter except the bad actor.

Captain swiveled his chair halfway around, looked at me sternly, and fired, "I'm only going to say this once! Help yourself to the fridge! Eat anything! Eat everything!"

"Yeah!" gawfed Tolstoy.

I'd waited for Captain to start pitching Jesus or Brigham Young or Amway. He didn't. I was fascinated. Were they actually just nice people?

"We're stopping in Pismo Beach for a few days," said Captain. "Near San Luis Obispo. Then on to Big Sur, Redwood National Park, and home to Medford. Medford, Oregon. Can take you that far. You can make camp with the fellows nearby. George there has been with us since Flagstaff."

Tolstoy banged the table with a big paw. Laughed. "I thank you!" he soapboxed in an Eastern European accent. "The people of Russia thank you! My mother and father! Smirnoff!"

"Pismo's fine, sir!" I shouted. I slapped roast beef and cheddar between sourdough. "I'll be headed up the 101 Salinas way."

"Right! Steinbeck!" he shouted. "Favorite Steinbeck book?"

"*Cannery Row*! Like *Sweet Thursday*, too."

"*Grapes of Wrath*!" Durocher called out. "That old Tom Joad was some kind of big."

"You?" I shouted at Captain.

"*Tortilla Flat*."

The twins untied the tonsils. Tweeted into each others ears. Twittered! Tore taffy! Bounced in front of us.

"Would you gentlemen like to sing some songs?" one asked coyly.

"Sure," I said. "Like what?"

Durocher winked a blue marble at the girls. "Know 'She'll be Coming 'Round the Mountain'?"

"Of course!" they yipped.

Everybody flapped their tongues. Even Bad Actor mumbled along. The twins had taken a shine to Durocher. Ten miles up the river, at Gaviota, they squeezed in on either side of the old nomad two bars into "Clementine." Butterscotch waved his arms, faking an orchestra conductor. Angelina awoke. Zipped his fly. Pulled out a harmonica. Stood up. Blew the accompaniment as we warbled.

An hour washed. Landscape Yellow Dye No. 5. Cardboard condos. Cadillacs. Velveeta sun. In the distance, virgin hills rolled to Neverland, immaculate, defiant. Then Santa Maria. Cow shit. Creameries. Captain pulled onto West Main along the periphery. Drunk Indians. Drunk priests. Government dreammakers buzzed across the desolation. We swung into a PO. Our door coughed open. Aunt Bambi handed junior to Captain, capered out.

Captain swiveled. "She's mailing a postcard," he said. "Anyone else?"

"Me," bawled Tolstoy. The bear got up with lustful eyes, followed Aunt Bambi's *Charlie*.

They returned in a PE. Captain passed junior to his wife, slid us back into the B matinee. Tolstoy plopped into his throne, spooked. His pinholes bounced between Bad Actor, Captain, road signs. I eyed Aunt Bambi. She had returned to her seat, her sparkle DOA. She leaned over Captain's shoulder, quietly jabbered the world was about to end. I saw it in her eyes. Did anyone else? The twins didn't as they merrily prepared a turkey sandwich for Durocher. My colon got a visit from Roto-Rooter. I heard Russian fight songs. Jailhouse queers. I peeped for a back door.

We made Guadalupe in a Hare Krishna chant. Ten worry beads south of Pismo. The vanilla roll lined with date palms, moonies, burger shacks. At a red light Aunt Bambi handed junior to Captain, took the wheel. Captain strapped the runt in a kid seat behind his wife, stuck a bottle in its mouth. The light changed. Aunt Bambi floored it.

Captain jumped up holding a two-eyed shotgun.

"Oh, Daddy!" screamed one of the twins.

Whoosh! Captain lurched to Bad Actor. Hovered over him. Pointed barrels at his chest. Butterscotch pulled his Yosemite Sam mask back down, ran and clung to Captain's leg. Bad Actor's eyes danced for an exit. His arms shot out like he was being squeezed in a trash compactor.

"George!" yelled Captain.

Tolstoy pounced on Bad Actor. He duct-taped the skunk's hands behind his back. The twins scurried to the baby's seat, sat over him protectively. Silence. I looked out the window. A sign read "Guadalupe Police Station." Aunt Bambi barreled into the parking lot, hissed brakes at the hive entrance. Thoughts of the FBI! Poor Howard! Othello!

"We saw his wanted poster in the post office," barked Tolstoy.

"Who is he, Daddy?" cried one of the twins.

"Donald Van Pelt. AKA the—a very bad man, sweetheart."

I stood up and slung the Kelty over one shoulder. "I'll be getting out here," I bugged. No one paid any attention.

"Me, too," said Angelina.

Door whisked open.

Captain flicked the scatter gun at Bad Actor. "Let's go," he said, and he slowly walked backward toward the door.

Tolstoy strong-armed the fugitive, shoving him along. The three oozed outside into the bright Velveeta. Angelina and I ghosted toward Aunt Bambi. She sat stunned, rock-a-byeing junior while the twins and Butterscotch fluttered around her. One of the girls took the baby, caressed it.

"You did good," I said to Aunt Bambi as I passed by. She didn't look at me, her hands weeping.

I dusted down the steps. Angelina shadowed me. Captain and Tolstoy marched Bad Actor past gawkers and into the hive.

Angelina foxed the RR tracks. I scampered half a mile north to the 1. Up ahead, a sign read "Dr. Zane's Discount Brain Surgery. 1/2 Off Special This Week!" Stood under a eucalyptus. Sun said noon. I fired a Swisher. Mused on the Winnebago scene. Wondered if they'd ever pick up another hitchhiker.

Pulled out my map. A hundred and fifty miles to Salinas!

19

Leaned Kelty against the mph sign. Propped "Steinbeck" on it. Siesta under the eucalyptus. An hour curdled. Rumble. A horn tooted. I looked up at a '70 Chevelle SS. Orange orange. Tornado belly. Ran to the window. An Asian smoke shook her red mane. Emerald-studded gold necklace. Black bikini top skinned small breasts. Faded Levi cutoffs. Guessed she was on the high side of twenty-seven.

"Going to Dr. Zane's?" she laughed, tipped her head toward the sign.

"Been. Got the special."

"And?"

"Feel incandescent."

"Hah!"

Ran eyes over her cherry ride. Her glam mug. "Women like you don't pick up hitchhikers. What do you want, Hi-tone?"

"Got a rape fantasy. What's in Salinas?"

"A rapist."

She laughed. Pushed the front seat forward. I tossed the

Kelty in back. Climbed in. The hellcat was perched on a stack of IOUs. I sopped up her s-curve. Five two, tops. White platform go-go boots tapped the pedals. She clutched. Threw a Diamond Hurst shifter. Roasted the tires. Fuzzbuster blipped on the dash. Ten-second quarter mile. A hundred mph.

"I'm in no hurry."

"Me, neither," she purred, fired a wanton grin, and gassed, "I just like to go fast." She balled the jack. A hundred and twenty mph! "Whew!" she cried. Slapped in Echo & the Bunnymen. "Four-fifty-four Turbo V8!" she howled above the music. "Cowl induction!" She glanced over, smiled, and cooed brass and whiskey, "I'm Sabrina."

"The Wanderer."

She chuckled. "What's in Salinas?"

"My confederate."

"A girl?"

"No."

She smiled with approval, fondled her necklace. "I'm from West Hollywood."

"Daddy own a gold mine?"

"Three," she tittered.

We rocketed by a semi convoy. Tongues! Horns! Hurtled past San Luis Obispo. Atascadero. San Ardo. She downshifted. Exited Highway 198. Grumbled along Cattlemen Road skirting San Lucas. All the houses built by Lego. I waited for her prop.

"Want to get a room?" she asked.

I set the ace of spades on her thigh.

Up ahead, atop a hot-sheet motel, a pink neon sign flashed "The Aztec." Sabrina pulled in. My adrenaline pinged. The Aztec was a tuna melt slapped on Chinet. Greasy fries. A cyclone fence choked a pool of horseradish. Pretty ringers, smeared with Coppertone, lounged around its perimeter sucking Bloody Marys. We coasted into the lobby. A sign on the wall read "Rooms available by the hour, day, or week. Pay in advance. No film equipment." A John Waters bit player slunk behind the counter. Queen of Gomorrah. Reptilian. On her third set of O-rings. She wore a body bag. Phony pearls. Sucker-fish lipstick.

Gomorrah fiddled with her hospital bracelet, nursed a Lucky Strike through a cigarette holder, purred sardonically, "Our suites are mid-twentieth century aardvark complemented with vibrating beds and prophylactic machines. I'm sure you'll find them adequate for your little rampage."

Sabrina plunked American Express on the counter. Her sneer slid off Gomorrah.

In the room, on the rattlesnake tabletop, Sabrina laid out coke rails that sparkled clear to hell. She was looking so fine, I lost my walking shoes. One hour. Booze. Two hours. Cooz. I'd fallen for a gypsy moth who flew too close to the flame. I was her two-day boy. The blues were going to rain. I didn't care. We crashed after the second gang of convicts jumped off the train.

We awoke at dusk. Ordered a pizza. Sat at the crummy table next to the TV.

"Where you headed?" I mumbled anchovies.

She piped with false bravado, "Got tickets for the execution."

"Huh?"

Her bravado curled into a Broadway smile. "Hector Ruiz. Tomorrow night. San Quentin's gas chamber. He pulled the shades down on two nurses from Santa Cruz seven years ago. Got an extra ticket. It's a cyanide seat. First row. Violent convulsions. Drooling."

"I thought only the press and family could—"

"Hector's my brother," she whispered. Her face dropped into a bucket of sulfuric. "My dad won't go. My mom died four years ago in Korea. She was from there."

Her dike broke. My fingers stunk. I held her like a piece of lettuce. We watched *Kiss Me Deadly*. Fell asleep at eleven.

Midnight. Awoke to crying in the crapper. Schlepped to the door. Locked.

"Sabrina? Hey, come on out of there."

More rain. I sat on the bed. Ten minutes dripped. She

surged out, fished for her bra and panties. Put them on. Lit a Winston and sat next to me.

"I've been in rehab for the past three months," she said. "I'm a sex addict. And a drug addict. Today I broke my vows to stay clean and uh, you know."

I was a disposable dildo.

She sat mute for another cig, found her gorilla girl.

"I started having sex with Hector when I was fifteen. He was seventeen. I seduced him. Four years later he murdered the nurses."

"That's not your fault."

"Hector was a virgin."

She blubbered. I needed a drink. A lobotomy. Linesman's gloves.

"That's not all," she whimpered.

I stroked her mane. Her head fell off. Rolled to *Let's Make a Deal*. Monty Hall stuck his cock in its mouth.

"I bought a nurse uniform," she cried. "And wore it many times for Hector before we had sex. He loved it. He loved it. He just loved it."

She killed the record. Chained another Winston. Cassandra screamed in my ear.

"I'll go to San Quentin with you," I said with reservation.

She put on a coyote mask. Black around one eye. "Really?"

"I need to stop in Santa Cruz first."

"Why?"

"My friend's circus will be there. I'm too late for Salinas. They'll probably blow tonight."

"All right."

After San Quentin, I'd make my way back to the circus. By then they would have moved on to Santa Rosa. If Sabrina couldn't take me, I'd hitch.

"After San Quentin, will you go back to Tinseltown?"

"Uh-huh. Come visit me on your way back south."

"Sure."

Sabrina scribbled her digits on a napkin. I filed it. We tooted up. Fucked to *Twilight Zone*. I drifted off at one-thirty as I heard her chopping more blow.

Sun up. I stumbled to the pisser. Locked again.

"Sabrina."

No answer. I went to the front window, yanked the drapes. Her Chevelle waited. I walked back to the can. Knocked hard.

"Hey."

I tickled the lock with a coat hanger, pushed swinger open. She was sitting against the shower wall. Hitchcock eyes. Her wrist, mortuary roses. Mack the Knife in her other hand. Checked the dancer in her neck anyway. No blips. I panicked. Shot out of there. Paced. Cried while cramming my clothes into the Kelty. Tried to piss, but couldn't with her there. Put the Do Not Disturb sign on the door. Slipped out.

I walked a mile north on Cattlemen to the 1 ramp. Pissed. Waved Steinbeck sign. Torched a Swish. No cars. Drifted in the horse latitudes. I was hungry. Sabrina's death scene looped. The projectionist ditched to Burger King. Set my mind on one of my idols, mopey ultra-cool actor Sterling Hayden. Five o'clock nubs. Rusty noir suit. Baloney sandwich shirt pocket. Pouring out dry monotone gems. Hell, if Sterling were in my shoes, he would've already forgotten about a dance with some suicide shrill at a hot-sheet motel. Who was I fooling? I was a chump. A fuck boy who'd fallen all the way in.

An hour floated. An International pickup swerved. Hiccupped sapphires. A silver Mexican stuck his head out.

"Soledad, mister," he said. Twitched his chin toward the bed.

I hopped over the side. Sat against the cab. Silver slid the cab window open, eased back onto the licorice. Hank Williams squawked on the radio.

Hank shut up after two more songs. An announcer's voice blazed, "Governor Deukmejian stated today that he will not grant a stay of execution for convicted murderer Hector Ruiz, who . . ."

Silver cocked his head a quarter turn. "Ever seen one?"

"No," I said. Sabrina's words echoed: *Come visit me on your way back south.*

"Oh, the gods who pull levers! Throw switches! The ones you never see. Men at desks for centuries. Scratching their greedy desires into the paneling with their fingernails." Silver waved a hand in disgust.

Thirty minutes croaked.

"I can let you off downtown," he hollered.

"Okay."

Silver dropped me on Front Street. I slopped bacon and eggs at a RR café. Bought a quart of Miller. Dozed for a few hours in an alley under a hangman's tree. Barking dogs flushed me out.

I choked a pay phone. Shook. Hallucinations I'd had of Pop at the Palace Theatre scraped and whirled.

"Mucklebird! Well, how's the French Foreign Legion?" he cheeked.

"Dreamy."

He chuckled. "Christ, you forget our number? Ever go to see Bolen in King City?"

"He played *Jeopardy* in San Diego after we talked."

"He know you're screwing his mom?"

"Wha—?"

"She got loaded at a Christmas party. Did a kamikaze karaoke. Said she was your 'weekend wife.'"

"I'm on my way to see my stepson now."

"Hah! Jesus!" He cleared his Howitzer, fired, "Word is the FBI are also after Bolen for the murder of a girl."

He let that hang off a cliff.

I finally flinched, sugared, "I called to, ah, I just wanted to hear your voice."

"So, you know about that. You're treading on pretty thin ice, aren't you, friend?"

Sabrina fisted me. "I'm okay."

"Bullfeathers. When you coming for a visit?"

"The Legion doesn't grant leave."

He laughed.

"Mom okay?"

"Always."

"I'll call sooner next time."

"Do that. Good luck."

20

Ten a.m. Soledad had the flu. Fever of 102. A Good Humor truck pouted under a maple. Chocolate Éclairs River hemorrhaged along the curb. I bird-dogged. Peered into the window. Filipino driver. Drunk. Lonely as a palm reader in Utah. Stuck his neck out.

"Somebody screwed the polar bear!" he slurred. "Reefer's busted!" He winced at the chocolate river. Shook his head. Tipped his flask of Mescal.

I walked away.

"Hey, *binata*!" he shouted.

I stopped. Turned. Good Humor waved a pistol like a dead pigeon. Images of Sabrina's corpse flickered. I didn't give a shit if he fired or not.

"Got two hundred bucks?" he pleaded.

He was bluffing. I spiraled. Rambled three blocks, to the Chapter Eleven Mall. Panhandlers. Pimps. Holy rollers. Darted into the freezer. Took an elevator to the john. Walked back toward the up-down—a hundred feet away. Anchovies squished inside. The doors began to pinch. A pipe cleaner toting a pink cake box whipped his horse. Streaked toward the closing doors.

"Come on!" he yelled over his shoulder at me. "They'll wait! Hold the phone!"

I clomped. Cake Box squeezed in between two olives. I slid in. The doors whisked shut. I glanced at Cake Box. Bald type-one engineer. He ogled a hot welfare momma. Tube-top. Three kids hanging possum.

"Someone's birthday?" she asked.

"My wife's head," he said matter-of-factly.

I half laughed. Half frowned.

"Degenerate," muttered a frump in a badger headdress.

"Betty's home today," a slouch whispered to his friend. "Should I give him our address?"

His pal, a rug doctor, snickered. Fuddled his combover. The doors hissed open at the ground floor. We poured out like a runny milkshake. Cake Box was first. He waited for me. I slung the Kelty over my shoulder. Ensenada toward the exit. He strutted peacock alongside me. Held up the cake box like a door prize. Passersby stared. I sketched the skinny. Doll's eyes. Cheekbones shrink-wrapped. Blue-red as baby rats. Vacuum mouth. White short-sleeved dress shirt. Plastic holder stuffed with pens. A compass. A tire gauge. Pits stained pumpkin. AC Delco name tag read "Stanley Pil." His waders were held up by a thin wallop belt like Pop's. From his hand dangled a plastic bag with sexy script: "Glitter's Lingerie."

Without looking at me, he asked, "Going north?"

"Santa Cruz."

"San Jose."

Revolving doors threw us over easy onto the oily tar.

"Can come along if you're not a homosexual or a Jesus freak," said Cake Box Stanley. He turned. Strolled through the parking lot.

I followed slow-mo. Eyeing the cake box. Side-stepping Silly Putty, neurotic housewives. Stanley approached a duck-shit-green AMC Gremlin. He crawled up its ass. I knew this prick was trouble. But I felt so unlucky as to be lucky. Terribly invincible. Depressed. I'd been Sabrina's fuck toy, her exit strategy. Wondered what Cake Box had in store for me. Bastard nearly dared me to ride with him. I had to see what was in that cake box. I snatched the Buck from the Kelty. Jammed it into the waistband of my pants. Opened the door. Propped the Kelty against the back of the passenger seat. Got in. Stanley set the cake box on the bench seat next to his right thigh. He tucked the lingerie bag behind it. Revved the motor. It purred like a blender of marbles. Goodyears spun. We waddled out of the parking lot to 101 North. Mute five miles. I stared at the cake box. Looked up at Cake Box Stanley.

"Special day?" I finally squawked.

"Yes, indeed," he said with a jackal grin.

"Wife or girlfriend in San Jose?"

"Ex-wife."

"Going to kill her, too?" I joked.

"If she's home."

"Come on! Lingerie and a cake. Anniversary or what?"

He tapped the cake box. Hummed "Jingle Bells." "Lingerie's for me."

Devil's food stuck in my throat. I rested my hand over the Buck. Eyes darted out the window. The valley floor sank a thousand feet on my side. Cake Box smelled my fear.

"Bug up your butt?"

"Can I smoke?"

"It's your funeral."

I turned to get a Swisher. Shoved the Kelty against a pile of newspapers in the back seat. The corner of a newly flattened pink cake box slid out! I grabbed a Swisher. Sparked. Kept mum.

"You know," Stanley capitulated, "I've been lying and have been told lies for forty-three years. On the job. At home. Everywhere! You're a liar! We're a culture of goddamn liars! And I'm the Christ almighty king!"

"I—"

Stanley jerked his head. Honed my eyes. Vapored, "I haven't lied to you yet, whatever your name is."

"Let me out at the next ramp! I mean it, mister!"

He stepped on the Gremlin's throat. Tee-heed. "What are you, anyway?" he scoffed. "Some kind of half-assed retro hippie out trying to 'find yourself?' On some kind of goddamn Injun vision quest?" He paused. Lost his smile. Daggered, "Really want to find yourself? Embrace death."

I scooted against the door. Pulled up my shirt. He eyed the Buck with indifference.

"Want to see what's in the box, don't you?" He tickled the lid. "Do you? Huh?"

"No! Yes!"

A faint siren! I stared out the rear window. Two cherries! Whipped cream! Stanley made goo-goo eyes in the rearview. Spanked the bugaboo. Ninety mph! He smiled down on the cake box. Waved a hand in my face.

"Pussy," he hissed.

I tore the lid open. Marilyn Monroe's head!

"That's Darlene," he said, dry as bleached bones.

I closed the lid. Puked on the floorboards.

"Take the Ray-Bans if you want," he chuckled. "She made great martinis. Nice tits. Couldn't stand Mr. Blink, that damn mynah bird of hers."

CHP cruiser scraped shit off Cake Box's door. Another tongued his tail. Christmas lights! Reindeer ahead! Cake Box stamped ants. We skidded like *Dragnet*.

"Get out slowly!" crackled the bullhorn. "Hands to Jesus!"

I complied. Cuffed. Stuffed maraschino. Visions! Infrared lineups! Charred corpses! Tigers! Peeped mesh. Stanley ossified. Hugged the cake box while dragged out of the car. Nightstick to the kidneys. We sped off.

An hour later in Salinas's hoosegow. Clearasil deputies Blind and Moby dragged me in. A Dillon and Sons Amusement poster with the same clown face as my postcard blazed on the wall. Othello's FBI wanted poster loomed opposite. They booked me. Alphabet soup. Formaldehyde. Cavity search. A new Boy Scout, Peach Fuzz, waltzed me to the fourth floor. I was dripping sweat and shit. They uncuffed me. Grabbed me with tongs. A dead kuromutsu! Tossed me onto the grill.

Turned the gas to high. The coals hissed. Steam. At the ten-minute bell, flipped me over. My nuts sucked. A tsunami washed into the interrogation room.

The budding Jap-Am detective said, "Surprised to get a slant-eye?"

"Only such a fat one."

He snorted like a sumo. Stroked his fifty-dollar haircut. Two-dollar tie. "I'm Detective Nakamura. We can do this dry or with Vaseline."

"How's Stanley taking it?"

"Dry as old snatch." Wonder Boy fished in his pants pocket. Tossed Othello's ten grand on the grill! Ben Franklin's mouth taped shut! Eyes screaming! Hiss! Pop! Othello's photo! The circus postcard! They must have found them, too! Married them, me, to his wanted poster?

I jittered, lipped, "Charges?"

He made eyes at Benjie. Smiled. "Working on it. Wendy upstairs is running the serial numbers. Maybe we'll hit the jackpot, like the press. Stanley Pil's going to sell a lot of motherfucking newspapers." He fanned his mitts over his head, spouted, "The Cake Box Killer. Nice ring to it, don't you think? And if Benjamin's digits come up cherries! Boy, oh boy! You just might get famous like your friend, The Pill."

"Ain't my friend."

Nakamura pocketed Ben. "We'll get back to this later," he said casually. Planted himself across from me. "Witnesses said they saw you enter the elevator at the Soledad strip mall with Mr. Pil. Correct?" He shifted his butt around on the chair like an Akita trying to shit down an anthill.

"You just antsy, or were you snorting in the evidence room?"

"Answer the fucking Q!"

"Yup."

He winked and crooned, "Helping him shop for lingerie?"

"Took a crap."

"Did you hear what Mr. Pil said in the elevator when asked what was inside the cake box?"

"Everybody did. 'My wife's head.'"

Nakamura slammed his fists on the prep table. Adolph's Meat Tenderizer flew. He tickled the heater in his shoulder holster. "Then why the hell did you get into his car? We got a two-hundred-dollar pool going on your answer."

I shrugged. "Thought it was a joke. Half the people in the elevator did."

"Damn! You've let me down, Michael. I bet you'd say, 'Stanley picked me up hitchhiking about a week ago. Let me stay at his house. Gave me Malibu ream jobs. Helped him box his wife for the church raffle.'"

"Fuck that."

"Now!" he blew testily, took a deep breath, paused, and meowed, "Tell me, when did you first meet Mr. Pil?"

"Today in the elevator."

"Stanley got a big dick? Is that it?" He stood. Lumbered. Lit a Camel. Tossed the pack under my nose. I popped one between my teeth. Sparked it.

"You're fishing for shrimp," I said. "Talk to the nutcase."

"Oh, we are. Know what he said?" He leaned over my shoulder, whispered, "He said that you were going with him to San Jose to do a Dunkin' Donuts on his ex."

"Lie!"

"Your prints are on the cake box," he taunted and straightened up like a Shabu dildo.

"I—"

"Did the packing while Stanley cut the missus's boobs off and made a TV dinner out of her mynah bird?"

"Fuck no! Let me answer, would you!"

Nakamura throttled down. Pecked his Camel.

"I opened the cake box just before your boys pulled us over. That's the fucking truth."

"Why?"

"He goaded me. I was curious. Wouldn't you have?"

Rising Sun blew a smoke ring big as a noose. "All right. All right. I'm almost half convinced."

Door banged open. Dust! Horse flies! Gold badge barreled in. Fresno Valley boy. Six six. Two sixty.

"Right on fucking cue," I muttered.

Studied the headliner. Goldilocks. Frito feed bag. Flypaper tie. Elephant gun in shoulder holster. Nakamura's eyes met his—Fresno shook his head, moved behind me. I was a T-ball waiting for the fat kid. Nakamura's eyes flashed signs.

"ID?" Fresno groaned through a mouthful of Fritos. Slapped my collar bone to the second floor. Nakamura tossed my DL on the grill. Fresno pawed it. Held it up to the fluorescent. Without taking his eyes off the DL, he said, "San Diego, huh? What you do besides moonlight as a baker's apprentice?"

"Union laborer. Local 89 in San Diego."

He bulled. Crammed my DL into his shirt pocket. Grabbed my hands. Turned them over. Looked at his pal, muttered, "Could've got those calluses choking the chicken." Dicks shrieked. Fresno stuck his Brut-redolent jaw next to my ear, asked, "How long you been Waltzing Matilda?"

"Week."

"Smells like a fucking year!" He stalked around the grill. Stood next to his pal. Sashimi chained another hump. I heard a zither! Screams! "Any destination, hot rod, or just drifting?" asked Fresno.

"Drifting is my destination."

"That's real goddamn poetic," he smacked contemptuously. Pulled his .44. Flicked open the cylinder. Clink! Clink! Clink! Three slugs dropped on the grill. "That's how many cakes Pil's baked," he blew and scooped up the lead.

Dicks seeped out the door. All the air was sucked out with them. I was a CPR dummy. A Dumpster full of tonsils. An hour jilted before another wave broke. Nakamura gushed in. Smelling like baby powder and gin. He perched.

"DA's got the hives," he gassed. "Ready to spill?"

"You do a good Joe Friday. Try a little more monotone."

He rolled his eyes. Bared his cig-stained pearls. "Let me tell you a little about Mr. Stanley Pil. Engineer at the AC Delco factory in Greenfield for twenty-three years. Only job he's ever had. Laid off two weeks ago, along with a dozen other lifers. Reagonomics. Bum deal—whatever you want to call it. Model citizen.

No priors. Belonged to the Rotary Club." Nakamura paused. Dragged his Camel. Yanked a chair. Propped a foot on it. Continued, "Stanley led the life of a dung beetle. Head down. Mouth open. Swallowed horse shit like nobody's business. His superiors rammed quotas and fear down his gullet until he was about as rebellious as a corpse." Detective circled the grill twice. Squatted. Ran a hand through Brylcreem. "His wife," he bled. "His late wife, Darlene. Kept Stanley in the toaster. Popped him up whenever she wanted to play Romper Room."

"And?"

"And apparently this morning, pending the coroner's report, Stanley boxed a Little Debbie for the third time in the past year."

"While I was crashed under a 101 overpass."

Nakurama threw Benjie back on the grill. Sweaty brow! Gaping mouth! They'd torn the tape off! Had Ben blabbed? Wonder Boy sized me up.

"What's a hitchhiker doing carrying a Vegas wad?"

"Insurance," I said coolly, knees knocking.

"For what?"

"Bail. Case some Deputy Dog wants to win the ring toss."

He chuckled lightheartedly. "Okay. Okay."

I was cold. I had run out of masks. Sabrina's "oh, no" flashed on my matinee movie screen, then the gas of hitching from Helix to the beach with Othello's seventy-five grand stuffed in a suitcase. Frames flipped from other hot rides. Then it hit me. Depression was me! Part of me!—forever! Not some entity dogging me. It made me what I was. Couldn't imagine what kind of person I'd be without it. It pissed me off, spun me reckless, yelled, "Hit me!" at the blackjack table when I was holding kings. Shined its fucked and divine light on life, that brief prize. During a stretch of sanity I always knew that D would loop, next time might take me down for good. So I sucked it all up— the road, the chances, the souls—desperate for one more taste.

Looked at the dick. "You asked me why? Why'd I get in Pil's car? Why the fuck not?"

"So you're a regular Mr. Fucking Excitement, huh?"

My shame lost its hard-on. I felt ethereal. Taoist. I laughed.

"No, just a joe who suffers periodically from clinical depression." It was the first time I'd mentioned it to anyone out loud.

He looked at me screwy, thought I was joking. "We'll see if Franklin's serial numbers sparkle."

"How long?"

"A day, maybe two," he said. Lit another Camel.

"Fuck!"

"And if we dust any of your prints at Stanley's home, well, you know." He cut.

I treaded water in the cesspool. Mulled. Did the San Diego Laundromat use enough starch? A cutie pranced in. Led me to a one-bunk VIP. The door slammed open. I walked in. Cold as cod. Ka-chink! Pressed snot between bars.

"A special holding cell," the cutie said, looked around, and whispered, "You haven't been formally charged with anything. Think you'll be okay." She smiled. Drifted.

I tumbled onto the bunk. Counted sheep. They trampled. Pissed. Got up. Paced Mexico City. The San Diego washer spun.

You've made another error in judgment, friend! rang Pop's voice.

Did they really miss Othello's photo and circus postcard? Fine police work! Insomnia slurred in my ear like a drunken whore. Fell asleep at three. At four I was rousted by the smell of Brut. Someone tied a pillowcase over my head! Cuffed me! Ripped my boxers off! Cold Vaseline. Steely Dan. A groaner. Salty ooze. Another cock. Smaller. Straighter. Fucked me longer. Harder. They left—quiet as friars. Sat numb. Dazed. Whirring black panthers. Fear. Howard materialized on the wall. Aqueous. Naked. Bloodhounds curling out of his rectum. "How sweet it is," he cracked and then evaporated. I stayed awake the rest of the night.

The sodomites never returned. I'd decided to keep mum. Feared if Fresno and company were ballsy enough to rape me in their own jail, maybe they wouldn't have too much trouble putting a bullet in my head down the line. On and off the grill for two days with Nakamura at the tongs. Fresno never showed again. Too busy cleaning my shit out of his dick. I still worried that the Jap-Am had played connect the dots with the FBI. Insomnia. Day three. Cutie came calling.

"We're releasing you."

"Jesus! When?"

"Now."

I jumped up. Covered with ash. Cum. Pig guts. Cutie led me to a caged window where a bulldog heaved the Kelty out. It was bruised, torn apart. I signed for my wallet. The stack of Benjamins. Still fat! Bulldog kissed me on both cheeks. Shoved me down its entrails. The door puckered. Crapped me to Seaside. Took a flea bath under a garden hose. Slung Kelty onto my back. The road! My temptress! My magician! My Judas! Gazed east of Eden. The Gabilan Range's pearly peaks! I bowed. Flung perverted Shakespeare verses. The brutes stood mute. The silence of kings! I humped the Natividad Road. Deadhead Old Stage Road. Gringo's black scar along *frontera's* periphery. Hurled through barbed wire! Chaparral! Into the rocky bosom! Fugitive fleeces flapping on the fences. I stripped. Raced naked! Throbbing! Skin afire! Red as Rio! My eyes jilted. Gushed a chorus line! Bounded up the parched slopes. Ascended the teats. The panthers! My lords! Red-tailed hawks! My angels! Camped under juniper boughs. Fires! Meat! Dance! I suckled coyotes. Sparred with windmills. Still I knew I'd never exorcise Salinas Jail.

21

On the third aurora, I bugged out for Steinbeck. 7-Eleven. Sign over door read "Free Tank of Gas with Purchase of any M-16." Bought an ounce of forgiveness. Six pack of Novocain. They didn't penetrate. Paraded to 101 North. Yanked out Othello's circus postcard. They'd be in Santa Rosa for the next two days. Pulled out notebook. Scrawled "Bourgeois Town" in retarded print. Thumbed. An hour greased. A '66 Plymouth Fury squealed tar. I galloped to the passenger window. Ernie, the Sesame Street Muppet, fondled the wheel!

"Hi ya, bud! San Francisco, huh? Me, too."

"You sound just like him."

Threw the Kelty into the back seat. Climbed in. Ernie floored it. Swung west toward Castroville, picking up Highway 1. I studied his striped shirt, the orange mask with the red nose and tuft of black hair.

"Is it hard to drive with the mask on?"

"Not at all. I do it all the time. So, Mr. Drifter, what's in the City?"

"Nothing. Want to walk across the Golden Gate." Didn't dare

mention Santa Rosa. Even Ernie might turn out to be a grifter.

"A real romantic, huh? I can take you as far as Hunter's Point near Candlestick Park."

A school bus rolled past. Giggling kids slid the windows down. Screamed, "Hi, Ernie! Where's Bert? Hey, follow us! Can you come to our school?"

Ernie waved and said, "I get that a lot. Everyone loves the Muppets."

"The costume?"

"A read-along gig at an elementary school."

An hour soared. Santa Cruz. Scott Creek. William Turner hung off the moon. Swabbing the sea canvas! Redwood fatties! Thought of Othello. Dead? Jail? Pin cushion? Ernie squealed onto the shoulder south of Half Moon Bay.

"Ernie's head's getting hot," he said. Bopped out.

Heard trunk open. Shut. Quasimodo appeared! Face! Melted rubber! Sliding off! I stared. Reeled! Gargled vomit!

"Pizza, extra cheese, extra sauce?" he warbled in Ernie's voice. Hopped in. Stabbed ignition. Eased back onto 1.

"I'm sorry," I whispered.

Five miles squished me.

"Hollister High prom king, 1970," Ernie finally said. "Car crash in Big Sur. I was showing off. Five years ago next month. I was in the burn ward a year and a half. That was the worst. I used to teach second grade. Loved it. Parents got me axed six months after I returned. They squeezed the school board. Said I was 'a threat to their children's mental well-being.' Oh, the kids! Kids are beautiful! After a while, they didn't see this, they—" Ernie began to cry. "The education system screws kids up. The cult of the hero! Teaches them hubris instead of how to guard against it! Makes them materialistic. Shallow as Death Valley."

"What's your name?"

"Cozumel," he said. Picked a pack of Kents off the dash. Flipped and lit.

"I'm Mike. Married?"

"The Prom Queen." His smile dried like plaster. "Two sons."

"Cool."

"Jim Henson heard about what I do. He wanted to sue me. Then he found out about my, you know, accident. Know what he did?"

"What?"

"Made this costume for me. Down in LA. Said he'll make me any Muppet I want to be. I'm thinking of doing Bert. Remember what I said about the kids?" His voice cracked. "Well, word's gotten around from Monterey to the Bay Area. Kids know the story about my face before I come to their school. They love Ernie. But they love me more! They make welcome signs. Give me gifts. Cards. Want to have their picture taken with me without my mask."

When he saw the tears in my eyes, he beamed the most beautiful smile.

He pulled tar in Pacifica. Donned Ernie's pumpkin again.

"Traffic's getting heavy," he sighed. "Rubberneckers. My headshot evokes strong responses in the City. Much stronger than yours."

"Uh-huh," I said, feeling no redemption.

"Been shot at three times."

"Really?"

"Once in San Jose. Twice in the City. Hey, I'm early. Where you want to go?"

"The Mission."

Cozumel dumped me at Eighteenth Street. I gave him a long aquamarine hug.

"Ernie! It's Ernie!" shouted a little Mexican señorita, tugging on her mama's coat.

I watched Ernie zoom away. Bought a Chinese smoke off a newsie. Torched it. The Mission. Pagans! Jugglers! Eunuchs! Jerry Brown hawking cardboard overcoats. Phony Charlie Parker fluttering bubbles. Gauchos filing their teeth. Italian dildos. Enema kits. I waltzed into Tino's All Nite Cafeteria. Cockfight crowd. Butch cake raffle. I smelled bacon. Farts. Illusions of grandeur. Shiny-mad Latino kids swirled like creek carp behind a butcher shop—swallowing people's hair. Eyes. Makeup. They go home and barf it up on their papas' work benches.

Pound out Zapata masks. I chummed next to a St. Louis dead-beat. Ex-wife in his throat—her Tenderloin au jus rivulet thighs. VD clinic punch-card in his pocket. A one-eyed drifter slob-bered on his shoulder.

"Ooh!" the drifter taunted. "She was a dandy li'l nubbins!"

St. Louis winced. Coughed blood, Beefaroni. Keds slung around his trembling Opie shoulders. He pawed his Lo-jo suit-case. Crammed with prayer tracts. Smut mags. Crinkled dreams wrapped in tinfoil. A Russian cafeteria lady foamed. Varicose veins. KGB pin. Stuffed doughnuts in St. Louis's RR pocket. An Italian beat cop washed in. Gut. Steam-shovel hands. Dali Lama twinkle mug. He ignored everything. Holiday whores. Caccia-tore priests. Hipsters in lumberjack shirts woofing roaches. Winos beating off on the radiator. Ordered joe, glazed doughnut.

"My dirty little rainbow," cop chuckled. Popeyed out.

Russian sliced a grin my way. Slapped down a trilobite. Magma fizz. Snot Dixie cup for St. Louis.

I catnapped in Dolores Park. Hit Elixir's happy hour. Betty Grable. Marvin the Martian. Longshoremen tattooing Goofy. Dirges! Merry jigs! Tears for St. Francis. Crashed among whale bones at Golden Gate Park. At Maypo, I marched across the Golden Gate Bridge. Triumphant. Plucky. Full of shit. Oh, glo-rious Golden Gate—the golden mountain's uterus! Mother of pioneers who'd cried out, "We've got scabs! Silverware! Sar-dines! I need you America!" Killers. Kings. Cunts. Holy Chi-nese. Robin Hoods. I loved them all. Gazed hi-ho. Spanish panoramas. Oh, America! Oh, California! Stolen. Regulated. But tramping makes me QT. Fuck fees, fines, licenses. The land cooing, virginal, threw me a wolf tit. Mountains! Sea! Deserts! I gazed across the bay, sucked fog. Blew kisses to the Atlantic. Found 101 roost, Marin County grade. Lit a Swisher. Pulled notebook. Wrote "Santa Rosa" big and black.

22

Made Rosie in an hour flat. A-bomb sandwich. Fishnet fries. Half pint of Wild Turkey. Snoozed with the pigeons until noon. Followed elephant shit to Dillon and Sons Amusement. Greatest Show in the West! Yeah, sure. Ferris Wheel spun a rainbow across the big top. Ambled with a dwarf up the midway. Smelled corn dogs. Cotton candy. Runaway pussy. Cut to the yard. A sea of dumpy trailers. Kinkers and roustabouts scurried. A blonde trapeze artist leaned against her old man's skeleton. Stuck a Lucky Strike in a hole in his throat. Suck! Wheeze!

"Looking for a kid," I said to them. "Mulatto. Wild eyes. Flamboyant."

"Chance," powdered the blonde. Smiled at the bones.

Skeleton pressed an Electrolarynx over the hole in his throat and roboted, "Follow the gunshots," and jerked his skull toward the runts of the litter.

"Much obliged," I said. Gatored toward scrap-pile trailers hugging the sideshow tents. Heard a gunshot over kid screams. Barking carnies. Lollapalooza music. A porkpie barker aped with a bullhorn. A reedy bastard plucked from a Charlie Chaplin film looked on indignantly.

"Come on, then, let's have it!" brayed Reedy. "The fat lady's water broke, and the goddamn cherry picker shit the bed!"

Porkpie inhaled. Stuck the bullhorn under his schnoz. Soapboxed, "The one-eyed wonder! Dillinger's pickled penis! Ladies and gents! Felines and fowl! Dillon and Sons! Greatest Show in the West!"

"More chutzpa, goddamn it all!" bawled Reedy.

"Jesus's birth certificate! Einstein's brain! Peruse our sideshow attractions! Freaks! Oddities! Killers! Beelzebub himself, ladies and gentlemen! That's right! Straight from Washington! Lepo the Leopard Boy! The world famous Frozo! Electricia! The girl who tamed electricity! Tonight . . ."

I wound through the sardine cans. More shots. Turned the corner. Othello's bare back thirty feet ahead. Shaved head. A tattooed bikini shook on some hay bales. A pineapple perched on her head. Othello raised his pearly pistol. Aimed.

"Christ! Can't you get someone else?" pleaded Bikini.

"Oh, Chance!" I called out, daffy. "Why don't you kids trade places?"

Othello spun. His ray gun found my tick box.

"Mike!" he yelled. Blasted two shots overhead. Ran to me. We hugged. He looked in fine feather. Off the meth? I didn't ask.

Bikini threw the pineapple to the ground. Misted into a nearby trailer.

"Don't mind the pie," he laughed. "Cardenia, the Illustrated Lady, ain't used to target practice. My regular ran off with a clown last week. Come on," he said, waving the pistol, and disappeared inside a Skoal tin.

I slid into the tin after him. King Othello sat at the kitchenette table. I took off the Kelty. Sat down opposite him. Scout poured slugs of Old Grand-Dad. We raised them and proclaimed, "Blood brothers forever!" We clinked and sucked.

Cardenia cakewalked in. Cunt up. A dashboard figurine. Cheekbones and cherries. Entire bod mapped with celebrity portraits. Roses. Disney characters! Guessed she was seventeen.

She donned a Yokohama robe. Sat on the sofa.

Without looking at his prize, Scout said, "Darling, why don't you take one of my heaters and go shoot the pecker off Boss Dillon. Bury it in his kid's mouth."

Illustrated laughed. Sprang up. Tied her robe. "I'll get some smokes," she said on her way out.

We toasted. Boasted.

"What do they call you?"

"The Durango Kid. Bullshit, huh?"

I fished in the Kelty. Threw the wad on the table. Othello's eyes puckered. He picked Ben up. Unfurled. Riffled like a deck of cards.

"Had your shirts cleaned," I said. Salinas Jail scenes movieola behind my eyes. "Cost you ten."

"The rest?"

"In Mermaid Mary's twat tuck."

"What?" he chuckled.

"Fort Knox."

"Can you get it wired to me when I need it?"

"Sure. Mermaid's an angel." I scribbled Mary's number on a book of matches and slid it to him.

"What took you so long to catch up with me?"

"Distractions." Sabrina steamrolled me.

"A girl, huh?" he winked.

The Q trickled from my wrist, dripped off my fingers. "Plan to stay with this gig?"

Scout squeezed Ben like a wet dish rag. Whispered, "Wolves are at the door." He laid the roll down.

"Saw your pinup."

"Popular, ain't I?"

"Give me all of it," I said. Poured a deuce.

Othello sparked his Zippo. Flamed my Swish. His Marlboro. "Blackmail's pretty raw business," he hissed. "There's a freak here, Prince Vivante, The Human Caterpillar. Used to teach college in Eugene. Born with no arms. Used to stick chalk in the cleft of his chin and write on the board."

"Fuck!" I laughed.

"A real hit. Kids took his class just to watch. He rolled in biscuits and gravy. Christ, they doubled his salary. Fifth year he began an affair with the Devil's sister. Fell in love. Thought she had, too. Oh, before that, his bed was a porn set. Banging coeds left and right." Othello paused. Shot a wicked smile.

"What?"

"Then the Devil's sister talked him into having his legs amputated."

"His goddamn legs? Why?"

"Right up to his nuts. Ta-da! To become a rootin-tootin carnival star!"

"The Human Caterpillar?"

"Right. She didn't talk him into it for the money, either. Sister had a fetish for quad amputees. Wanted to bounce on Caterpillar's dick like a pogo stick. Promised she'd marry him and be his forever da dee da."

"And sister gets tired of it? Takes a powder?"

"Uh-huh. Christ, wait till you see him. Caterpillar's bitter as bug juice. Angry as Adam. And wants my hide."

"Jealous of you and your harem?"

"I guess," Othello said, rolled his eyes, sang the first few lines of "I Shot the Sheriff." Scout flicked his cig ash on the linoleum, cracked, "Fucker saw the FBI poster a few weeks ago. Wants five grand."

"You got ten."

Scout lit another smoke. "Let's squash him before he turns into a butterfly and flutters to the feds."

"Fuck! No!"

"Card game tonight after the show. Caterpillar's always there. I'll tell him I have the money. We'll take him to the dump. He has no family. No friends. Not even a goddamn dog! Freaks will think it was a suicide. Hell, he gets lit and spews about killing himself all the time!"

"What about the next freak who sees your pinup?"

"Carny folks ain't rats, generally. Christ, most are on the lam or running away from one kind of hell or another."

"Give him five tonight. See if that shuts him up."

"If it doesn't?"

"Then we'll explore all the colorful options."

"Fuck, Mike! Mr. Pragmatic! Jesus, okay."

Cardenia reappeared. Threw smokes and an Oly six pack on the table. Dropped her robe. Shook off her bra. Fried liver and onions. I faked dreamland on the couch—worrying! Watching through slitted eyes as Cardenia gave Scout head. Grand-Dad spilled on her back. Scout was ready to kill tonight! The cavalier way he talked about acing Caterpillar made the New Mexico murder parboil my brain. Had he killed the girl? He said he hadn't, but he was so fucked up on meth at the Helix house I still wasn't sure.

Five rolled around. Scout donned a red western shirt. Blue neckerchief. Fringed pantaloons. Yanked on cowboy boots. Holstered Colt Navy twins. Reminded me of his Union scout duds—the night he whacked poor Howard. We escorted the Illustrated Lady to the sideshow alley.

"Elvis's rubber!" bulled the porkpie barker. "Ladies and gentlemen! Kings and criminals! Baby Venus! The smallest woman in the world! She lives in a shoebox and is married to a gerbil! Tonight only! Free admission for clergy! Degenerates! Witches!"

Cardenia dropped her robe. Slid into a glass booth. A swarm surrounded her! We continued down the alley. Passed Millie-Chrissie McKoy—the Two-headed Nightingale. Flamo, the Human Candle. Minus, the Cow with No Legs. We reached a lone shitbox trailer.

"The Caterpillar's?"

"Wait," Scout said. Flapped the dog door.

A muffled shout, "Well, the half-breed killer!"

Othello barged out five minutes later.

"Okay?"

"That fucker's never okay," he muttered. "Come on!"

Stamped through beef flaps into a swollen tent. From backstage, we looked out on a thousand saints in blue seats. Othello twirled a dervish. Shot the nipples off the Statue of Liberty. Applause. We toured the boss yard after the show. Queen trailers. Walked into one, the lounge car. Plush! Freaks perched around a card table.

"Chance!" yelled a crimson man.

Othello turned to me, whispered, "Lobster Boy," and yelled back, "Hey Maine! Time to bend over."

I followed Scout to the bar.

A low-cut babe on duty. Python coiling around her neck. She gave me the eye, asked, "Who's the freak?" Everyone laughed.

"IRS!" barked Othello. Grabbed two Dos Equis. Handed me one. He sauntered to the card table, sat next to a kid who resembled a chimp, pomped, "The freak's my brother."

Eyes lit up.

"Mucklebird," Othello said, and pointed his beer at the snake lady. "Miss Opal, The Snake Enchantress. You met Lobster Boy there with the mouth. Gondio, the Boy with the Monkey's Head. And Twisto, the Girl Contortionist.

"Caterpillar showing?" chirped Gondio.

Twisto pouted. Muttered, "I say we stuff the worm in a bottle of Mescal."

"Let's toss him off Desolation Bridge," cawed Miss Opal. "See if he turns into a butterfly."

Door swung. Othello's lemon, Cardenia, waltzed Vegas, grabbed a beer, shouted, "Some townie tried to stick his finger up my ass!"

"Give it back?" asked Othello.

Everyone roared. She winked at Scout. Sat between him and Gondio. Petted the boy's monkey skull.

Lobster busted out a new deck, shuffled, and crowed, "Five to play."

Everyone tossed a Lincoln into the pot. Scout was glued to Cardenia. I jimmied in next to the monkey boy. Lobster tossed the cards. A sputtering wheezing sound outside.

"The Human Caterpillar," someone groaned.

Door squeaked. Sussex strongman! Burly Garson! Succulent mustaches! Nutty tights! Carried trouble on a platter. Caterpillar! The human rump roast! Wrapped in yellow cellophane. Purple loincloth. Burly stopped next to Twisto. Set the platter on the table. I gawked. No arms! No legs!

"About time, small fry," said Lobster Boy.

Caterpillar grinned. "Hooker swallowed my minnows."

"So suave," chided snake lady.

While massaging her cards, Twisto picked the worm up with her feet and set him on a low chair next to her. He leaned his belly against the table.

"Smoke?" he asked.

Othello sparked a Marlboro. Tossed it on the table. Twisto grabbed it with her toes. Stuck it in Caterpillar's mouth.

"Thanks, Negroid," he mocked.

Othello's neck veins popped. His six-guns!

I turned to him, asked him without saying a word, *Blanks, right?* He smiled coyly. Hit his beer.

Without looking up from her hand, Cardenia asked, sugary, "Did anyone hear about the little guy who cut off his goddamn legs for a dame? For love, no less."

Suppressed chuckles. Othello vamped her neck. Caterpillar smirked, probably thinking about the five grand. Plucked the pots for the first hour. Couldn't take his eyes off Cardenia's willowy branches. Got drunk. Rubbed his cock against the table. Second hour. Worm in the red. He watched jealously as Othello fondled the Illustrated Lady.

He glared at Twisto. Barked, "Drawers," and nodded.

Twisto dipped her toes into the worm's Saran Wrap. Fished out Scout's blackmail. Flipped it onto the table!

"Is this how much a dead girl's worth in New Mexico?" Caterpillar asked. Ran his eyes over Cardenia's tits. "Or a man from St. Paul? Fucking five lousy thou!"

The room fell silent. Eyes danced from Othello to Caterpillar.

Miss Opal caressed her boa with both hands, glared at Caterpillar, scolded, "We know about the wanted poster, Worm Boy."

Scout marveled. Puffed up.

"Families stick together," drawled Lobster Boy.

"*Mi hermano,*" yipped Gondio.

Twisto toed Ben. Set him down under Scout's whiffer. Othello pocketed the roll. Pulled Wild Bill. Aimed at Caterpillar's antenna.

"Wimp!" goaded the quad.

"Do it!" yelled Cardenia.

"Illustrated's been fucking me for a month now," spit Caterpillar. "She's just thick enough to believe I'd split the twenty-five K reward with her."

"Liar!" screamed Cardenia.

Scout pushed his chair back. Drew Wild Bill's twin. It found Cardenia. Her celeb tattoos shrieked. We all jumped up. Plastered the walls.

"Send me to Jesus!" taunted the worm.

Door blew. Siamese twins Ping and Pong Fong, the Two-headed Boy. Stuck their necks in.

"Mr. Chance, police you trailer," stammered Pong. "Plenty hornet."

"My trailer?"

"Man. Pretty woman. FBI," Ping said.

Othello's eyes grabbed mine. He holstered his pistols.

"Run!" hoarsed Twisto.

We scrammed into the shadows out the back door. Vaulted chain-link. Tore up an apple orchard. Scout pulled up. Bent over, hands on knees. "We'll circle round," he panted. "Wait till they're done licking my sardine can. Sneak in. Get the rest of the loot. What you think?"

"Okay," I said.

The Kelty! In Othello's trailer! Othello's photo, his circus postcard: my Bastille ticket! It would sing to the judges! To Pop! He'd beat me to Belfast. Summon the galloglasses! Wolfhounds!

We scraped our hips along an old limestone wall. Cut back toward the circus. Pomp! Pomp! Crept through the sardine yard. Hid in a clump of Judas trees. Scout's trailer was full of lightning bugs! Yard boss chomped his stogie out front. Hands on hips. Dick Tracy cutouts flashed in the windows. Fed bumbled out.

"Mr. Shinebox," I whispered. "FBI who showed at the Helix house a week after you."

Sara Lee strutted. Vexed. Sexy as edible panties. Flapped jaws with other two.

Scout's tongue wagged. "Shiny's partner?"

"Sigmoid Agent Sara Lee. She was at Helix, too."

Helix scenes tumbled dry. Flo Bolen. Braless. Shrieking. I couldn't look at Othello.

Five minutes waxed. The Gypsy oddity called Ocean to Ocean poked the trio. Pointed in the direction of card-game trailer. They hoofed dust. We jittered another ten. Bolted. I grabbed the Kelty. Othello plucked Ben. A photo of his dad. A box of Remington cartridges. Jeans. T-shirt. We ghosted into the black.

"Train yard a mile," whirred Othello. We whipped our bang-tails. "We'll circle north of Old Town. Jump there."

Boiled alleys. Barking dogs. Yakking kitchens. TV shows' milky blinking lights. Scout halted after four furlongs. Shed his red shirt. Gun belt. Pantaloons. Pulled Ben. One Colt. Stuffed the rest of the Durango Kid into a trash can. Slipped into his T-shirt and jeans. Stuck his pistol down the front. I fished in the Kelty. Pulled out the Cal map. The postcards. The Buck. Stuffed them in my pants. Pushed the Kelty on top of Durango's duds. Closed the lid.

"Bluebirds will be scratching the Greyhounds," I tipped. "Train yard, too. Do a Goldilocks?"

Scout nodded. We zigged northeast half a mile. Pregnant pear orchard! Swooped into the harvest shack. Plunked down on the wood floor. Scout yanked his pony. Flicked the chamber open. Slid in three zombies. Laid it across his shank.

"You really going to shoot Caterpillar?"

"Jezebel, too," he muttered without looking up.

"Cardenia? Bullshit. How do you—"

"Her eyes," he hissed. Shook his head. "Her eyes sang Johnny Rotten." Slammed the pony to the floor.

Scout's scene at the Helix house ran me over. I couldn't hold back. "I want to hear it again now that you're off the Drano. Did you kill the girl in New Mexico?" I caught him on the jaw. "No."

I blew lungs to Los Alamos, smiled meekly. "Sorry man, I had to make sure. I'll never doubt you again."

We hugged the silence. The circus scene played across the dark wall.

"When the three bears going to show?"

Scout looked off as if I hadn't peeped. "Alaska's the land of the midnight sun," he clucked wistfully. "Light all summer. Damn near twenty-four hours a day. Did you know a man can still homestead in the forty-ninth state? Imagine that!"

I started singing Lennon's "Imagine."

Scout caught my eye, crooned along with me, then he looked away. "Some kind a world, huh? Beauty like John Lennon gets shot up. Shit." He sparked a cig. Dragged. Smiled. "Find a piece of land. Erect a living shelter. Some kind of other building like a shed. Dig a well. Live there seven years, and you own it outright."

"How many acres?"

"A hundred. A fucking thousand if you want!"

"Damn!"

He jumped up. "Gold about everywhere. Northern lights. You get to kill a moose each fall for the long winter. What do you say?"

"Homestead in Alaska? Jesus, Othello! I don't know. All that goddamn snow. Dark for six months." I clammed, torched a butt, purred, "I'll see you to Fairbanks."

"You and me, amigo," he yipped. "I'll take anything Alaska dishes out," he boasted. "Maybe the only place I'll ever find peace." With that, his bark faded. He dropped like someone chopped off his legs. "Howard appears to me," he whispered.

"His ghost?"

"Plain as you sitting there. Wearing that damn Shriner's out-fit." He paused. "Maybe he won't follow me to Alaska."

"You don't believe that?"

"He talks to me."

"What's he say?"

"All kinds of mumbo jumbo along the lines of, 'You got it coming.'"

"Maybe you need one of those hoodoo conjurers?"

"Maybe I need the electric chair for him to leave me alone.

Last week he came to me in broad daylight while I was target shooting. Broad goddamn daylight! In a hoity-toity tux, with a walking cane. Blood all over his head just like that night. He cried, 'If you're any kind of man you'll put a bullet in your head. You should have known we were acting.'" Scout's sad eyes searched me for a reply.

"Fuck Howard," I said. "He had it coming. What you did was self-defense. What you did was heroic."

"It was murder just the same. And I ain't doing no jail time for first degree or second degree or whatever damned degree the FBI coonhounds got in store for me."

"You could spill about Howard. I'll testify. Maybe a lawyer can find other kids the Shriner and Genie flimflammed."

"Lawyers," he gawfed. "Shit."

"You want to run forever?"

He smiled and sprang up. Slipped out into the orchard. I followed. We plucked pears.

23

We waited for the three bears. One Mississippi! Two Mississippi! No claws! Othello pitched Alaska nonstop. I knew he had the pluck and the wits to make it homesteading. I hoped the hard-luck kid would make it up there. I hoped he'd find peace and come to terms with that awful night in St. Paul. As much as I wanted to, I couldn't give him that peace. I couldn't save him, either. He'd changed. I'd changed. I'd never been much of a follower, but I planned on seeing him to Alaska, wherever he wanted to settle. Just didn't know how long I'd stick around.

We skedaddled at dawn on the second day. Crept across Santa Rosa's north side. I flashed my thumb on the 101 while Othello hunkered in the weeds. Hour! No fish! Finally, a '51 Buick Special. Raspberry red. A Jehovah's Witness hanging off the grill. Zinfandel pouring out three-holer ventiports. Ran like mad! Electric window hummed. Silvery Audrey Hepburn! Blue-on-blue polka-dot dress. Angel food hat. She smiled.

"Healdsburg. Fifteen miles. Your friend hiding in the weeds

can come, too."

I waved the high sign. Othello dashed. Scooted in next to me in the back seat. The Special glided. Audrey quietly studied us in the rearview. Three miles blipped. Jehovah's Witness fell off the grill. Thump! Thump! Under the wheels.

"Oops," she laughed. Her rearview eyes found Othello's.

"What are you boys doing out in broad daylight? Together, no less?"

We bugged mute! Her eyes skated mine.

"He's on TV. And there's a pretty accurate description of you, 'mystery man.'"

Scout pulled the Colt. Cocked it. "Please, ma'am. Let us out here."

"Is that how you display your gratitude, young man?" she gently scolded. "Oh, I don't believe half the nonsense I see on television. Put the pistol away. You can stay at my house."

"Oh, sure!" moaned Othello.

Audrey bruised the brakes. The tires cried! Smoked! She twisted. Threw on a hag's face. "I taught English at Crenshaw High twenty-five years. Tangled with characters of every stripe. You're quiche at a chili contest. Now, in or out, bub? Make it quick!"

"Okay! Okay!" whined Othello. Shoved the Colt back into his pants.

"That's more like it," she mewed. Smiled. Turned back around. Gassed the rasberry.

I elbowed Scout's ribs as we passed a sign that read "Cat Ovens 2 Miles."

"My daughters, Rachel and Catherine, are vagabonding around Europe," she chirped proudly. "Kind of like you boys. George and I worry about them day and night. Hope they meet nice people. Guess you could say I'm looking for an edge. For some good karma for my children."

Scout and I cracked nuts. Nothing popped out.

"You call it," I whispered. He shrugged.

"Now listen," Audrey piped, "my husband will throttle me if he finds out I picked up hitchhikers! And oh, how he—!"

"Hold it!" I howled. "He won't mind you dragged a couple of delinquents home? One wanted for murder? As long as they weren't hitching?"

"George's funny that way."

We roared.

"George'll be home around five. So, we'll tell him you boys walked into the beauty parlor in Healdsburg and asked for directions. He knows today's my hair day. And I gave you a lift, okay?"

"Sure," I chimed.

"Okay, lady," Othello added.

Audrey shot us a sneaky smile. "George is at the hypnotist," she baited.

"Really?" said Othello.

"Trying to break his Ken-L-Ration fetish."

"The dog food?" I asked.

"Promise you won't say anything to sweet George," she doved. "He's sensitive as a Trojan Ultra-Thin."

"We promise," Othello tittered.

"A year ago George brought home two cans of Ken-L-Ration. Liver and Tender Chunks. I thought it was a joke. After all, we don't own a pooch. After the girls went to bed, he opened a can, dumped it in a pan, and heated it up on the stove. Fried three eggs and mixed them in. Ate the whole thing with toast and coffee."

"Jesus!" I laughed.

"Try any?" asked Othello.

"Not that night," she giggled. "George performed this ritual once a week. He didn't understand why."

Othello asked, "Did you try to stop him?"

"Are you kidding?!" she hooted. "We started having the best sex we've had since LBJ was president!"

We cackled.

"Do you believe in past lives?" she asked. "I do."

We shrugged.

"Well, Dr. Dick, his hypnotist, is convinced George was a war dog in World War I—grandsire of none other than Rin

Tin Tin!"

"Fuck!" I laughed.

"I can't wait to meet George!" yawped Othello.

"Oh, I think you'll like him," she creamed. "He's a wonderfully humble man!"

"You said you didn't try the Ken-L-Ration *that night*," I said.

"Oh, yes!" she bubbled. "One night around two a.m. I found George nude in the kitchen on all fours. His face buried in a bowl of Tender Chunks. His favorite."

We laughed hysterically.

"It turned me on like nobody's business! So, I stripped. Got down there with him. Growled like a cat. Planted my kisser in the bowl, and we polished it off together! You can imagine what ensued."

"Uh-huh," we said.

A cop car blurred by, flipping us back to our *Dragnet* episode. Twenty minutes pulsed. Scanned for more cherries. Winged monkeys. Audrey exited 101. South Healdsburg. Churned dust on the dirt road. Quarter mile. Powwow trailer. Double-wide. On the Russian River. Lonely. We birthed. Lady crushed Othello's toes. Stuck out her hand.

"The flamethrower," she demanded.

Scout looked at her sideways. "I'll be naked," he groused.

"We'll all be naked."

He obeyed. Bowed.

"You, too," Audrey said.

Handed her the Buck.

"Why don't you boys go for a swim. I'll holler when lunch is ready," she said. Vanished inside the fat man.

We danced eyes. Shrugged. Moseyed down the slope to the Russian. Othello whirled. Scrutinized the Sleepy Hollow scene.

"She's calling the coppers!"

"No, she ain't," I said. Stripped. Swan dived. Surfaced. "What's really eating you, frieeeeeend?" I snickered, mimicking Pop.

"A twenty-year stretch."

"Not everyone's an asshole." I told him about the Winnebago family, Ernie.

"I can't do no ball-and-chain." He slumped on the bank. Didn't budge. Twenty minutes skipped town.

"Lunchtime!" yodeled the lady.

We scampered up the slope to a picnic table. Dagwoods. Potato salad. Baked beans.

"Now, what are we going to tell George?" the lady asked.

"We want some dog food," Othello smacked. Barked.

"Uh, that we came into the beauty parlor in Healdsburg," I said.

"Asked for directions," warbled Othello. "You gave us a lift."

She grinned. Wafted back through the slider. "If you want more, holler. Come on in and watch a movie after you're finished."

"I say we vamoose before George comes home," Othello mumbled through spuds. "He might not be so benevolent."

"Let's give him a chance."

He chewed on that for half a ham and Swiss. "Fuck, okay."

Went in. Lounged in recliners. Watched *The Sting*. Snoozed. Awoken by sounds of George coming home. The lady was spinning our agreed-upon lie. We jumped up. Shaky. Ready to bolt. George floated ethereal. Prince of the redwoods! L. L. Bean poster boy. Fifty. Skin-and-bones. Specs. Cue ball. Pictured him bare assed on linoleum. Face buried in Ken-L-Ration.

"Hello, rascals," he said, smiled big. Extended his hand.

I shook first. Othello followed.

"Brewskis?"

I nodded.

"Sure," said Othello.

"Bunny, three Buds, please." He sat down at a little card table next to the kitchen.

We aped. Bunny slung sweaty longnecks. Grabbed Jack off nearby bookcase. Three shot glasses. Poured. Killed. George torched a cob pipe. Leaned back.

"We don't need to hear whether you guys are guilty or innocent of any crimes," he said. He smiled at Bunny. "Damn fascists running the show." Poured another round. Raised. Shouted, "For liberty and the lost frontier!"

We threw down.

"We're escapees ourselves, aren't we Bun?" he said with a wink. "Got the hell out of LA's boob machine a few years ago. After Cath finished high school. Retired early at fifty-five. Bunny did, too."

"What'd you do?" asked Othello.

"Fortune Cookie Writer."

"Really?"

"Weally!" he laughed.

"What's your favorite fortune you wrote?" I asked.

"Build a bomb shelter. Now!"

We giggled.

"Tip wisely. Your waiter is an escapee from a hospital for the criminally insane," said Bunny.

"Funny," laughed Othello. I laughed, too.

Bunny squeezed in next to George with a photo album. "Our girls," she said. "Rachel, twenty-three, and Catherine, twenty-one. Two months ago. Before they left for Europe." She whimpered.

George clutched her hand. Said proudly, "Bought them Eurail passes. Unlimited travel anywhere in Western Europe for sixty days. Oh, they've done a fair share of hitchhiking, too, to meet people and experience the local culture. Been to half a dozen countries already—Belgium, the Netherlands, the UK. They called from Madrid Sunday last."

"How long they been gone?" asked Othello.

"Twenty-nine days," said Bunny.

"I'm sure they'll be all right," I said reassuringly.

Killed off Jack. Slushy toasts for Abe Lincoln. Elvis. The '60s. G-spots. Apollo 11. Slinkies. Girl hitchhikers. Othello and I slabbed in the recliners and watched *Lost in Space*. Saviors stumbled into their bedroom for an Afternoon Delight.

Six p.m. George waltzed into the living room in a bathrobe. Half a hard-on.

"Going into town for dinner and a little mamba. Be back around eleven. You fellows help yourselves if you get hungry. Twin beds in the girls' room. You don't have to wait up."

They left at seven. We watched *The Honeymooners*. Played Cootie. Whoopee Cushion.

An hour spit. We lounged in the recliners. I cut the TV.

"Your Long Beach postcard," I said. "What were you doing there?"

"Thirty days."

"For what?"

"Vagrancy."

"And?"

"Public drunkenness."

"Rimbaud would've been proud. Bluebirds in St. Paul and Cal didn't chew. You got lucky."

He chuckled.

"Before that?"

"Living with a pie in Huntington Beach. Tan Line Tammy. Wore scuba gear to her first porn tryout. Hole in her arm like a whirlpool. She walked after we shacked for six months."

"The seventy-five grand?"

"Didn't get it selling Bibles."

"Blow?"

"Shit pays out like a fucking Disneyland vending machine." I fired off a sermon about Lance Ryan's demise.

"Want to be my savior?"

"No," I lied. "Someone on your trail for the loot?"

"No."

"Shit."

"Someone was. Heard they were walking Jesus."

"You send them there?"

"Hell no!" he squawked and buried that card. He opened a new deck and honeyed, "What you been doing in Diego? Have a girl?"

"A ninety-pound jackhammer."

He laughed.

Sabrina's reel spun so hot the projector died. "See a few beach girls."

"No one special?"

"Uh-uh."

"Come on!"

"A cougar picked me up hitching on 101 a few days ago. Real nice. Fiery. We went to a flop. Killed herself in the crapper while I was asleep."

"No way! Fuck! Why?"

I rattled about Sabrina's brother's execution, the extenuating circumstances. Didn't mention Salinas Jail. Had deep-sixed the lockbox containing those scenes.

Lights out at 9:30, Pooh beds in girls' room. Insomnia gnawed. The Winnebago family! Technicolor! George and Bunny highlights! My reels flickered on a cruddy black-and-white at Desire Motel. Gazed at Scout. He penned his epitaph. He saw himself as a gallant motherfucking romantic. Othello the swashbuckler, gliding above all the shit, just like in school. I wondered if he wouldn't mind dying.

Roostered at eight. Bacon and eggs! Oh, Bunny! Oh, honey! Our swank den mother! Othello slipped five Benjies under the pillow. Stuffed the rest back in his pants. We paraded into the kitchen. Bunny was slinging four burners. Mother Goose robe. Hoppity-hop slippers. George already at the feedbag. We bellied up to the trough. Platters of bacon. Jimmy Dean. Scrambled eggs. Short stacks. Toast. Marmalade. Skippy. Pitcher of OJ.

"We're leaving today," I said.

"Oh, you don't have to!" called Bunny. She hopped over. Set down a frying pan full of hash. "Try it," she winked. "It's the George special."

We gaped. Ken-L-Ration! Horse balls! Pig hooves! Bovine snot!

George grabbed a spoon. Plopped a dollop on our plates. "Good enough for Rin Tin Tin." Leaned back. Laughed.

"I told George I told you boys," said Bunny.

"You don't have to try it," said George.

Othello swallowed a forkful. Yucked snobbishly, "Swine nose, with a wonderfully long caramel finish."

We all chuckled.

I straightened up. Made big eyes at saints. "We've been a

hell of a load on you."

"Well, if your hearts are set, how about tonight?" asked George. "I'll take you to the train yard on the north side of town. I'm assuming that's how you'll be traveling, since you're keeping a low profile and all."

"We'd be much obliged," I said.

Hung out all day. Played Barrel of Monkeys. Mousetrap. Bunny won. She whipped up a king's lunch. Dinner: T-bones. Sweet potatoes. We planned to sally at ten. Everybody went mum around nine. The saints were worried. I counted rosary. Othello counted bullets. George flung me a pair of pants. Shirt.

"Promise I'll burn your getaway duds," he said.

Ten ran up on us. George gave Othello his thunder stick back.

"Oh, Jesus! I hate goodbyes!" cried Bunny. She bear-hugged Scout. The hard-ass choked up. Bunny gave me Bucky and a bowling bag. "There're four ham and cheese and four roast beefs in there. And a Thermos of coffee." She hugged me. "You keep Othello in line, Mike, okay?"

"That'll be the day," I said, teary. Crammed the California map into the Dunlop.

Christ, we hugged forever. Sticky as rubber trees! To the point of suffocation! Perversion! Ghosted George's Ford 150. Bunny winced away from the powwow. The prince pussy-footed the pedal. Highway 101 turned into *The Wolf Man* set. Fog fumed. Weird racket rattled the brambles. Queefs! Sloppy braying. Bedlam screeches. Headlights caught Lon Chaney Jr. crashing through the woods! Bursting out of his shirt! Frantic! Halfway to Crazy Town. Bear traps snapping at his feet. He yelped. Misted. We rolled dough around a hairpin turn.

Half a bag of popcorn later, George scraped the Southern Pacific yard's ribs. We said goodbye. Spied for gung ho bulls. Cinder crunchers. Clear! Tap danced along the tracks. Sprang into a freight car. Two bearded hobos already inside. Sitting on orange crates. Passing balloon juice. A Spanish candle between them. A cold pot of gandy gumbo. Thunderbird snored at the other end of the car. King-sized feed-sack blanket. A

Greek fisherman's cap veiled his face. The beards threw us Missouri stares.

"Oh, kind gentlemen of the road, to which locality dost this coach fly?" I asked, smiled, and bowed.

They gaped. Snorted approval of my asinine delivery.

"Well, Mr. Jack Wanderlust," gawped one, "Eureka via Ukiah with transcendental views of the Russian River."

"Along the Eel River through wee Willits, radiant Redway, and fair Fortuna! Then on to Portland!" the other bellowed, took a snort. "Where a bad actor cut Shorty Gleason ear-to-ear over a bottle of monkeyshine!"

They cackled.

"Old Shorty was some jungle cat!" roared number one. "A dirty little ringtail if there ever was one!"

"I'm Fly Away Jim. He's Fly Away Jack," said number two. Othello jerked his head toward Thunderbird.

"The Tooth Fairy," Jim said. "Hopped day before yesterday. Hasn't mumbled a word. Who you Flintstone kids be?"

We didn't reply.

"Lot of that going around," said Fly Away Jack. He looked off, a heartsick face.

"Sit, road kids," Jim said. Pulled his beard. Fidgeted.

We sat across from the blackbirds. Our backs rubbing the wooden slats of the car. Jammed Bunny's bowling bag between us. A bush baby stuck its head out of Jim's coat pocket. Orange hoodoo eyes. Jim looked down. Rubbed the little man's head with a greasy palm.

"This is Dixie Joe," he piped. "We guess he's around a hundred years old. Drinks a bottle of beer every day."

We smiled. Eyed the bush baby. Jim ran his orbs over our bag.

"Going to eat snowballs?"

"Nah," grunted Othello. "Going to see my sister in Seattle," he lied.

"We're tramping to Spokane for the apple harvest next month. This rattler will die in the Portland yard where you can nail a red ball to Rainy City."

Jack continued moping. Jim studied his brethren. Looked

up. Softly muttered, "Our angelina got clipped by a midnight creep."

"Your what?" Othello shrugged.

"Their protégé," I whispered.

"And some protégé Silas was," Jack blued. "He'd been with us a few years. We keep him safe all that time, and then he goes and gets himself killed. Last night, a lone freight car drifting through the yard. So silent he didn't even hear it come up behind him."

"Sorry to hear that," said Othello.

I nodded.

"He left like smoke," said Jim. He looked down. "He flowered into a real fine American nomad." Covered his face with his arm. Cried. A minute later he pulled a harp out of his ragged duster. Blew "Swing Low, Sweet Chariot." The moon swelled!

"Silas turned one-six last November," Jim said and palmed the harp. "Tried to coax him to leave the rails. To go back to Oklahoma to his kin—"

"Hell!" muttered Jack. "His father throttled him. Ma ran off. We were his family."

We sat in silence. The train rattled out of the yard. We jawed on and off through Cloverdale. Ukiah. Fly Aways drifted off around midnight. The Laytonville water tower flickered. I checked Thunderbird. Still zee. I pulled out the Cal map, butterflied it, laid it on top of the Dunlop bag.

"Should reach Eureka by daybreak, then another seventy miles to the Oregon border," I whispered.

"Then how far to Portland?"

"Two hundred. I'm guessing. Like Fly Away said, in Portland we'll jump another freight to Seattle."

"Then we should hitch to a local yard just south of the Canadian border, hop a rattler that'll take us across. We don't want to play kissy-face with border badges. We'll hit up tramps in Portland for the local yard info."

"Sounds Siamese. And do the same at the Alaska border. Hey, we need to scrounge British Columbia and Alaska maps."

"Uh-huh."

Othello pushed the map aside and pulled out two sand-wiches. Handed me one. I stuffed half a roast beef.

He bit into his. "Let's cut the pie, Mike," he whispered, and pulled Ben's wad. Set it on his lap. "Safer that way."

"Jesus Christ," I hissed, gazed through the ink at the other riders. "Put it away."

Scout quickly slid the map over it. "They're asleep."

I ran eyes over the snowmen, Thunderbird. Quiet and still.

"Five each," he said.

"Too much."

He peeled five grand. Stuck it under my nose. "Take it."

I grabbed the boola, crammed it into my pocket. "Thanks."

Scout slipped his wad back into the Dunlop bag. I crabbed to the boxcar's open door. Swung my legs over the side. Moon and stars were showing off! Scout scooted next to me in the doorway. We kept our eyes on the others. Rode mute for two Marlboros.

"Howard billowed last night," whispered Othello.

"What'd he say?"

"'Twenty-three,' over and over."

"Twenty-three what?"

"Age I die?"

"New Mexico girl ever show?"

"Time to time."

Othello picked up the Cal map. The Thermos. Poured. "Sleep," he said. "I'll keep a lookout. We'll switch in a few hours."

"Okay."

I shuffled inside. Leaned against the wall. Faded to black. Raucous dreams tumbled. I was being chased through the woods. I was naked and fat. Shiny and blue as a butchered hog. My limbs and torso blown up like the Michelin Tire mascot. Bloodhounds brayed. Some asshole repeated my name through a bullhorn. Scout nudged me around four.

"Where are we?" I whispered.

He picked up the map. "North of Rio Dell. About fifteen miles south of Fortuna. Eureka, an hour at most. Christ, I can smell the Klondike, Mikey!"

I stood up. Stretched my bones. Walked to the door. Pissed outside. Dawn crept in. Misty moon. The freight crawled around a sidewinder.

"A shooting star!" I whispered loudly. Jerked my head toward Scout. He hopped to his knees. Caught my eye. I turned back toward the show. "Another and another! Quick! Scout, you got to—"

I heard a thwack. Something tearing. Whoosh! Othello came crashing into me! We plummeted. I looked up falling. A blurry Thunderbird stood in the door. I landed hard and rolled down the gravel slope. Looked up again. Son bitch flashed a jackal smirk! Waved Othello's wad of Bens like a pom-pom. Squeezed the Dunlop bag to his belly. He ran to the opposite door. Jumped! The snake's tail a mile long. The Fly Away boys appeared in the doorway. Gazed down. Wide-eyed as lost kids. Held out their arms. Othello was next to me on the ground, eyes closed, still. Bloody shirt! I lifted it but saw no marks. Turned his head. An ice pick at the base of his skull. Seeping like mad. I shook my friend.

"Othello! Scout!" Nothing. Blood-drained. Dead? It couldn't be! I cradled his head. "Oh, no! No! No! Oh, no!"

I was an orphan. A Siamese with a dead twin. Stammering prayers. Obscenities. I bellowed out the play-by-play of Othello's death scene over and over—I would change the ending—save him. But he only ended up dying ten different ways, and each time, I watched so helplessly. Imagined the ambulance blazing. Sirens. Apathetic attendants chucking Scout in back like a trash bag. I dragged his body under a fir. I closed my eyes and saw Othello on his Sting-Ray. Glen Lake blacktop radiating, sunny July. Topps flapping in his spokes. My *fidus Achates*! My Tom Sawyer!

I paced—spied up and down the tracks. No Zephyrs. Only wilderness. My mind boiled. Sputtered. I couldn't think straight. "Run! Run!" screamed the frantic kid inside me. The cops! The FBI! They'd haul me in. Pin Othello's murder on me. I deserved it! For doubting him about the New Mexico murder! My witnesses were ghosts. Fly Away boys only existed in the gentle fires between life and death. They'd never be found. Howard's killing! The FBI wanted someone's hide. I was the only one left. I had to run. My wings—hacked off. Dripping steam oil! Sulfuric. My ribs shivved! Fillets for fairies. I heaved Othello's corpse. Warm mercury. Ooze. Lugged it to the rails. Osiris waited. In ostrich feathers. With a red hard-on big as a crook. Laid Scout down next to the tracks. They'd find him there.

Walked east down a fire trail. No map! Heavy as if I were still carrying him. Stopped. Looked back. Tears. Couldn't go on without him—but somehow did. Redwoods embraced me.

24

Tramped through the cathedral. Three miles. Highway 36 gleamed. Stripped off my bloody shirt. Hurled it into the weeds. Flashed my thumb. A freightshaker slid past. Airbrakes wheezed. Tail lights blinked hello. I dashed. Door popped. A vanilla sundae. Three scoops. Pine nuts. Extra fudge. Cherry on top.

"Boise," Sundae mumped. Cracked a smile. Rayed Black Beauty eyes. "Hauling king mattresses with a bum back. Help me unload, and I'll throw in a shower and a steak dinner at a truck stop."

I gripped my hips. "Last trucker propped me wanted a BJ. Sent him to TJ."

"Hah!" he laughed and then bugged serious, "Well, there, sonny, you ain't my type!" Laughed.

"Okay, mister." Climbed in.

"Burrow in," drawled Sundae. Threw gears. "Thirteen hours."

I sank, hissing like a deflating blow-up doll.

Sundae reached back into his sleeper. Pulled out a T-shirt

that read, "Melanin-Impoverished." Tossed it into my lap. Chuckled, "It's you."

I slipped it over my hollow shoulders. We drifted through Trinity National Forest. Le beau idéal! Redwoods spit hot coals at my head. I longed for ravens! Worms! Maggots!

Fir glared. "Watch your friend's back!" sneered the Adonic bastards.

Mile markers ticked off, Mexican crosses. One for every one of Othello's years, Howard's. Hades choir. Sang filthy tunes! Cunts of Cimmerian shade! Hurled arrows! Cockroaches! I looked over at Sundae. Fat slob was going to do me in! Slit my throat! Rape my rotting carcass! Had it coming.

Picked up Highway 299 to Redding. Caressed by the sandman. Dreamed Mermaid Mary. My naked banker! The OB Flynns! My Irish brothers!

We reached the Boise factory at seven p.m.

Sundae nudged me. "Pay the piper."

I pissed on a bird-shit Reagan statue. Took an hour to unload Sealys. Then we followed a meth trail to Old Faithful Truck Stop. The sound of clanging metal. A hundred silver fish under twinklers. Burly drivers dry-humped fenders. Bragged up their rigs. Vets tiptoed around with their VA checks. Looking to score junk. Bearded deacons passed out Jesus tracts. Inside. Red. Plush. Angus cadavers. Suckling waitresses. Steak. Hot shower. As Sundae had promised.

I bought a roll of quarters from a corsage-smile cashier. Waved Sundae goodbye. He lit out for Vancouver. Out front, a greasy pay phone. Palmed the receiver. It stung! Could barely hold it! Thought of Flo at the Helix house. I'd deprived her of seeing Othello one last time. I dropped in the slugs. Ringing. A mute pick up. I heard violins! Gnawing rodents! Stilettos sharpening!

"They're all dead!" Mrs. Bolen finally slurred.

"Flo."

She was bawling. "The FBI called half-pitcher of martinis ago. Goddamn it all, Mike! Othello was my, my—"

"He didn't suffer." Guilt. Piss. Pause. "I was there."

"You were there, Mike! Goddamn it! You're always there, Mike! Mr. Lucky! Mr. Lucky shit! I'm sorry! I'm sorry!" Sobbed some more. "What the fuck happened?"

"Bushwhacked on a freight train."

Bottles clinked. "Where are you?"

"Purgatory."

She blurted, "Bastards finally caught the killer of that New Mexico girl. Believe that?"

"Johnny Sample?"

"Right. How the hell long have you known that?"

"Long enough for you to hate my guts."

She slurped through tinkling ice. "Oh, Jesus!" she cried. "It doesn't matter now. The FBI has been trying to pin that damn rap on Othello for years! Damn cops! Slow as molasses! Fuck! They've officially called off the dogs, Mike. You can quit running."

"I'd like to believe that."

"It's true. Now that Othello's with angels, both the St. Paul coppers and the Fibbers have closed the stinky book on Howard Strum's murder."

"Uh-huh," I said. Waited for the anvil to drop.

Flo crushed jalapeños. "Did Othello kill that man?"

"Yes."

She gasped. Whimpered.

"It was an accident. Self-defense. He was being courageous," I said. "He thought he was saving our lives. This guy, Howard Strum. Was an actor from the Guthrie. You probably knew that."

"They told me," she slurred.

I told her the story. Gasps. Sniffles. Long silence.

"I'm flying out to San Francisco in the morning. Want me to identify—" She broke down.

"I can't say how sorry I am," I mumbled. Paused. "Expect a call from Western Union."

"What the hell for? I don't want any of your or Othello's drug money."

"Don't know where he got it," I lied.

"How much?"

"About five Cadillacs."

"Used or new?"

"Fifty-five grand."

"Jesus!" she cried. "Okay, send it. Maybe I'll go to Europe. Or buy a cemetery plot for myself. Where you going to go?"

"Baja, for a while, maybe. I don't know. I'll head back to SoCal eventually."

"Othello ever know about us?"

"No."

"Want to see me?"

"Always, sugar."

She choked up. "You call me when your legs get tired, okay?"

"I will."

"This mess, Mike—Othello's death—it isn't your—" her voice trailed off. She stormed tears. Hung up.

Hooked the receiver. Cried. Slid out of the booth. Slithered into the 7-Eleven. Salted pumas. Crow sandwich. Red beer. Black magic marker. Moped back to the conch. Snitched a collect call.

"Walsh's."

"Pop."

"Michael!"

"Othello's dead."

"Jesus! How?"

I spit Walt Disney.

"I haven't had that much smoke blown up my ass since I got a call from a Reagan campaign solicitor," he said when I finished. "Where are you?"

"Boise. Could you take a visitor for a week or so?"

"Need scratch for a plane ticket?"

"I'll hitch."

"Sure?"

"See you in a week."

"Good." He clammed, finally whispered, "I'm sorry about your friend."

"Thanks."

Sparked Zippo under a Highway 95 overpass. Black widow webs! Humped south a half mile to the next Hilton. Made my death camp. Chanted raw vows. Lies. Phony litanies. The night carved holes in me. Othello's five grand flipped me off. Considered copping out on Land O' Lakes. Pop's strap-o-lounger! The Inquisitor! Sure he was charging the batteries. Testing the cerebellum probes!

Six a.m. Stumbled onto the ramp, 95 South. 84 East. They rolled out to Mirage! Detention. Solitude's bleak house. Road crew raking fresh blacktop! My muse! My mentor! An eternal pageant of actors, scenes, and I got to play a part! I whirled! Caressed her wicked lines! Caught my breath. Leaned against the sign: "95 South—Reno 420 Miles. 84 East—Salt Lake City 341 Miles."

Mexico via 95, or 84 to Mom and Pop and the family? Lit a Swish.

My innocent winged child lit on one shoulder. Othello's bloody angel on the other. Stabbed me! Brooded. Hurled tiny thunderbolts.

"Wanderer!" the angel cheered.

I grinned, found a piece of cardboard. Scribbled "Redemption." Stood on 84. Flashed my thumb.

www.ingramcontent.com/pod-product-compliance
Lightning Source LLC
Chambersburg PA
CBHW060224180626
46813CB00007B/2952